AIRDRIE

OCT 11 2012

D0014862

PRAISE FOR
DARK EDEN

"DARK EDEN is a fast-paced thrill ride. . . . A compelling read that transposes the best aspects of classic horror storytelling onto a modern backwoods adventure reluctantly experienced by seven terrified teens." —*Los Angeles Times*

"A spooky, psychological thriller. With seven different characters who have seven different fears, there is bound to be someone for readers to relate to in one way or another. . . . The supernatural twist at the end will leave teens with more questions than answers." —*School Library Journal*

"Engrossing and deliciously unexpected, DARK EDEN is a tale that slithers across our skin, a cool breath on the back of our necks that raises the fine hairs and has us frozen in place, held immobile by the paralyzing fear of turning around and facing what's there." —*Supernatural Snark*

"This book blew me away. The big 'revelation' was jaw-dropping and utterly fantastic." —*I Just Wanna Sit Here and Read*

"DARK EDEN was quick, clever, and completely satisfying." —*Bookish Brunette*

"Patrick Carman's new YA novel is a sure winner."

—*Between the Pages*

"DARK EDEN was just pure awesomeness."   —*IceyBooks*

"The star of this book is the setting. Carman has created an austere landscape where a new horror lurks around every corner."   —*The Well-Read Wife*

"DARK EDEN had me hooked in the first few sentences."

—*The Page Turners*

"Carman excellently plays up the creepy factor in DARK EDEN, with an eerie setting and lots of tension. . . . You never know who might be lurking around that next corner."

—*Novel Novice*

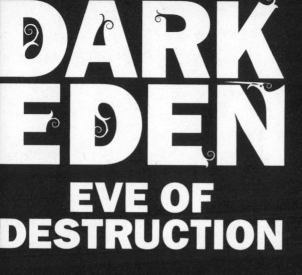

DARK EDEN
EVE OF DESTRUCTION

PATRICK CARMAN

Illustrated by Patrick Arrasmith

Katherine Tegen Books
An Imprint of H

AIRDRIE PUBLIC LIBRARY
Bay 111 304 Main St. S
Airdrie, AB. T4B 3C3

Katherine Tegen Books is an imprint of HarperCollins Publishers.

Dark Eden: Eve of Destruction
Text copyright © 2012 by PC Studio
Interior illustrations copyright © 2012 by Patrick Arrasmith
All rights reserved. Printed in the United States of America.
No part of this book may be used or reproduced in any manner whatsoever without
written permission except in the case of brief quotations embodied in critical articles
and reviews. For information address HarperCollins Children's Books, a division of
HarperCollins Publishers, 10 East 53rd Street, New York, NY 10022.
www.epicreads.com

Library of Congress Cataloging-in-Publication Data is available.
ISBN 978-0-06-210182-2

Typography by Joel Tippie
12 13 14 15 16   LP/RRDH   10 9 8 7 6 5 4 3 2 1
❖

First Edition

For Karen
Until death do us part

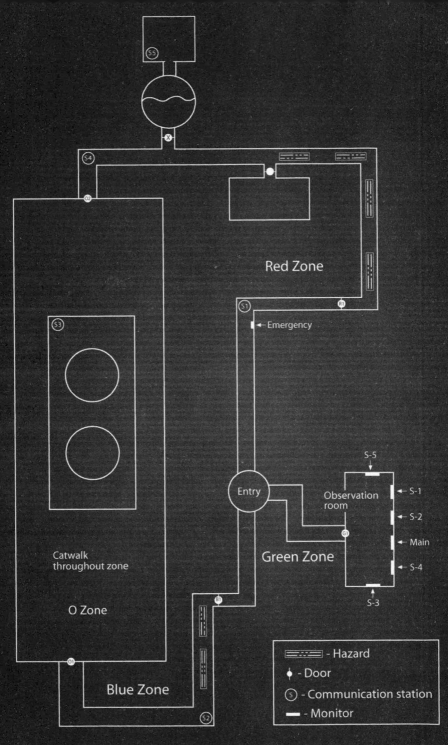

MISSILE SILO MAP

When a man has outlived his limit, plunged in age, and the good comrade comes who comes at last to all, not with a wedding song, no singers dancing, the doom of the death god comes like lightning. Always death at the last. Not to be born is best when all is reckoned in. But once a man has seen the light the next best thing by far is to go back, back where he came from quickly as he can. For once his youth slips by, light on the wing, light headed, what mortal blows can he escape? What griefs won't stalk his days? Envy and enemies rage in battles, bloodshed, and last of all, despised old age overtakes him. Stripped of power, companions. Stripped of love. The worst this life of pain can offer. Old age, our mate at last.   —Sophocles

This man will die. I will see to it. He will wish he had never been born.   —From the notebooks of Eve Goring

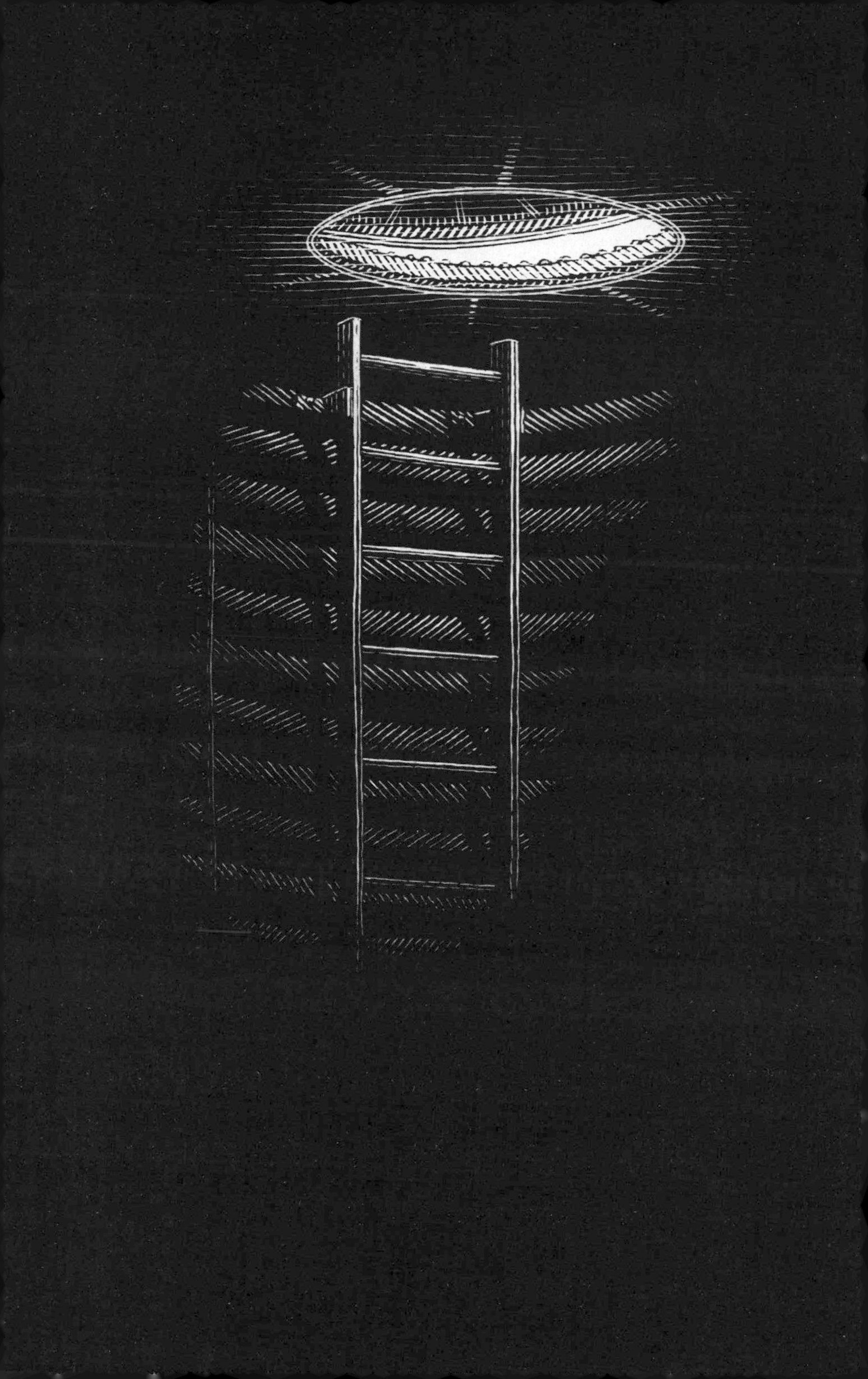

ATOMIC
UNDERGROUND

A year after I left Fort Eden, Mrs. Goring sent me a message. It came through Dr. Stevens, whom I hadn't heard from in a long time. There was no return address on the envelope, so she must have hand delivered the note while I slept, then slinked off into the darkness like my neighbor's cat.

I found the letter by accident at 2:32 AM because my lawn had been forked, a middle-of-the-night prank that had become popular among my friends in recent months as we'd all gotten licenses to drive. Turns out going to school leads to meeting people, so there are now four or five guys that I pal around with. Who'd have thought it? Me, Will Besting, loner of all loners.

Forking involves a lot of plastic tableware, usually around five hundred white forks, stuck in the victim's front yard. When my friends were done, they dropped all pretense of secrecy and laughed, slammed car doors, and sped away. My hearing isn't what it used to be, but I'm a light sleeper and my window faces the street. I got out of bed, went to the second-story window, and saw their taillights as they rounded a corner.

My friends think forking is a fabulous prank, but when I looked out at all those white ends sticking up under the streetlight, my yard looked like a scale model of a military burial ground.

It wasn't funny.

It was haunting.

I crept downstairs and found a plastic grocery bag in the kitchen, went outside, and stared at the cemetery that had taken over my parents' lawn. Picking them out of the grass wasn't easy, because all the white ends of the forks had been covered in slippery Vaseline.

It took a long time to remove all the forks. Standing

there in my shorts and T-shirt, I glanced at the mail-box and the street in front of our house. The mailbox reminded me of what I once was: a lonely, scarred kid; a kid who wouldn't go to school; a kid without his brother. And the mail carrier made sure to remind me each and every day that I was home alone: *Slam! You hear the sound of this mailbox being shut? That's the sound of your life closing in on you. Get used to it, loser.*

I walked to the garbage can on the side of the house and put the heaping bag of slippery forks inside. The clinking sound of many plastic things settling into space was distant, unhearable, and a familiar new fear rose up my chest and into my throat.

It's getting worse.

Walking to the front door, I knew it was true. I'd left Fort Eden cured of one thing and plagued by another. I could still hear, but not the soft things, not things like five hundred plastic forks falling against one another. As the months passed, it *was* getting worse. I was hearing less.

When I reached the steps to the house and looked down absently, I saw the letter, its white corner poking out from under the doormat. A few minutes later, settled back into bed with my Recorder in one hand and the letter in the other, I read it out loud in a whispery, three-AM voice:

Hello, Will. We haven't spoken for a long time, but I've watched you from a distance. I can see you're doing just fine, and it makes me happy. Thank you for getting well. You were my last patient and it's nice to know I didn't end on a low note.

As you know, there have been some complications with my practice. I've moved on, moved away, moved forward. Don't try to find me, Will. I can't be found.

I know you don't remember very much about your cure at Fort Eden or about Rainsford, the man who cured you. And you probably don't have much memory of Mrs. Goring, the woman who maintains the property. The way the cure works, as you know, leaves some empty spaces in your mind.

Mrs. Goring has asked me an unusual favor, one I hesitate to bring to your attention. I wouldn't contact you at all if it wasn't a last wish.

She's dying, Will. Dying of old age and she won't come out of the woods. She knew I could bring you all together, or that I could at least try. She wants to see all of you once more. But mostly you, Will. I have no idea

why, only that it would mean a lot to her if you could
gather the seven and go back.

Back to Fort Eden, where you were all cured.

On the seventh day of the seventh month, early in
the day.

She will be waiting.

All my very best. I do miss our chats.

Cynthia

I had four flashes of insight when I read the letter out loud. I'm funny that way. Hearing the words in my ears, no matter how soft the sound, is different from only reading them in my head.

The first insight: *She doesn't know.* Dr. Stevens had no idea Mrs. Goring told me the truth about what happened to us. She doesn't know that I know *everything,* all the darkest secrets of Eden. If she did, she'd never attempt to send me back.

The second insight: *Dr. Stevens is no longer practicing medicine.* I knew she had vanished under the weight of so many questions. All of us had come back from Fort Eden with our fears erased, but we'd also returned with new ailments that would never go away. For me it was my hearing, which was maybe 60 percent of what it once was. Ben Dugan got arthritis, Kate Hollander blinding headaches. Alex brought back legs that fell asleep if he sat in one place too long, Connor brought the first stages of senile dementia, and Marisa, my sleeping beauty, can't be trusted to drive a car because there's a reasonable chance she'll fall asleep at the wheel on her way to school.

The third insight: *Mrs. Goring has forced her daughter's hand.* All I could think was that Mrs. Goring told Dr. Stevens she'd better deliver this message or else. Mrs. Goring would have the power to do that like no one else. *Get them down here or I'll tell everything I know.*

And the last flash of insight: *The seventh day of the seventh month was seven days away.* I had to hand it to Dr. Stevens and Mrs. Goring, they were good at aligning numbers.

I stared at the ceiling in my room for half an hour, and just before drifting off to sleep I felt my subconscious piecing together a weird version of how things might go down.

Mrs. Goring wouldn't die after all. Our visit would, in fact, revive her. Enough so that she'd elude us in the woods while playing a round of hide-and-seek. By the time I found her napping in the trunk of my car it would be too late. She would take up residence in my house, play my video games, drink my Mountain Dew, watch my TV.

And then one day I'd come home from school and find her standing on the porch with a bloody ax in her hand.

Sometimes I despise my imagination.

====

The next morning I made a futile attempt to contact Marisa. With summer well under way she rarely stood up before noon, so trying to find her at ten AM was a complete waste of time. I sent four or five texts, called her cell, called her house, and pinged her Facebook page, which said she was online even though I knew it was a total lie. She worked afternoons and nights at Dairy Queen, so there was a sliver of time when I could actually talk to her—usually from noon to about two PM—after which the whole cycle started up again. Work from two to eight PM, home to bed, up at noon, repeat. This was the reason I was ringing Marisa's doorbell at 10:30 AM the morning after I got the letter. Her mom answered the door and let me in. A delicate woman with an olive complexion and a Spanish accent, Mrs. Sorrento was endlessly in a rush.

"When she wakes up, make her take the vitamins, yes?" she told me, gathering up her purse and yelling to Marisa's younger sister about chores and computer time (do the chores, cool it on the computer).

"No problem," I nodded, stepping inside but not closing the door. Marisa's mom was getting ready to leave anyway, and a nice morning breeze was in the air, cooling the un–air-conditioned entryway.

"Bang some pots and pans," she said, taking up her keys from the counter with a metallic swish my ears barely registered. "That usually works."

Mrs. Sorrento and I got along well and she trusted me, mostly because the other boys Marisa had brought home were jerks that, according to Mrs. Sorrento, only wanted one thing from her daughter. I'm not sure I should be happy about this—that I'm considered a safe boyfriend by Marisa's mom—but it doesn't bother me any. She left the house and I played video games on the TV with the volume cranked, hoping to wake Marisa. Fifteen minutes later I walked down the hall to her room. She was indistinguishable from the blankets and pillows, quiet as a whisper. I said her name, but she didn't stir. When I crossed the room and sat on her bed, leaning down to find her soft breath, she spoke.

"Get in," she half whispered, and I knew what she wanted. She was trying to lure me into a warm embrace in which she could fall back to sleep.

"Can you get up?" I asked, touching her gently on the shoulder.

"Do I have to?" she asked. "What time is it?"

I lost my will to sit on the edge of the bed while such a beautiful girl summoned me closer, and slid in next to her, whispering.

"It's only eleven in the morning," I said. "But I need to talk to you."

"You drove all the way over here?" she said, and I could tell I was losing her to dreamland by how she mumbled the words close to my ear the way she always did. She knew how to speak softly and be heard.

"Dr. Stevens sent me a letter," I said. "Mrs. Goring wants us to come back."

Marisa turned in my direction, blinking awake. "If I didn't know better, I'd say my mom put you up to that to get me out of bed."

"No, it's true," I said, pushing the dark strands of her hair aside. "And I think we should go."

"You're serious?"

"Yeah, I'm serious," I said.

Now she was awake, lying on her back, staring up at me.

"Just you and me or everyone else, too?"

I kissed her gently, listening to her sister on the phone in the background. When I pulled away, she smiled.

"You have puppy breath," I said.

"That's what you get for waking me up."

And then she asked me again: "You and me or everyone else, too?"

"She wants us all to go back. Will you help me round up the troops?"

"If you make me some coffee, I'll think about it."

She pulled me closer, kissing me with more assurance than I had kissed her, then groaned and sat up.

As she got herself together, I made coffee and went back to my game, exterminating aliens with some sort of gun that shot green flames across the screen. I thought of my brother, Keith, and how he would have blown me out of the water if he were still alive. And I thought the same kinds of things I often did when I found myself lucky enough to be in Marisa's general vicinity when she was awake.

I love this girl. I should have saved her from the cure. I should have done a better job kissing her.

"Smells good," she said, sliding across the kitchen floor on pink flannel socks.

She picked up her phone and began texting.

"Who first?" I asked, knowing Marisa was already getting down to business.

"I'll put Kate on the job. She'll get it done."

Kate Hollander was the most forceful of us all, but I hadn't talked to her since leaving Fort Eden. If Marisa could get her on board, everyone else would be a snap.

"Where should we meet, what time, what day?" Marisa asked when I set a big steaming mug of coffee in front of her.

I told her we should go early because the drive was long. And we'd need two cars for all six of us.

"I can carry three or four, see if you can get Kate to drive, too," I said.

An hour later Marisa and Kate had rallied Connor Bloom and Alex Hersh. I got Ben Dugan, who hemmed and hawed with excuses until I told him everyone else was going. He caved at the idea of being the only one left out, and we had the group.

Kate Hollander, Connor Bloom, Alex Hersh, Ben Dugan, Marisa Sorrento, and me, Will Besting.

The only one missing from the original seven was Avery Varone, the girl who feared death above all else.

We had no idea where she'd gone.

Seven days later I stood at the edge of a trail and felt the black power of Fort Eden drawing me down into the shadows of the wood. A year had passed and many things had changed, but not this place. The realm of Rainsford remained the same.

"It feels like it did before," Ben said, staring down the winding path while he wrung his hands nervously.

"Only hotter," said Connor. He was eying Marisa with interest, a situation that made me wonder how many girls he'd stolen from lesser men than me. He was right about the temperature. It was hot, like 90. It would be cooler down below.

He moved his gaze to Kate and threw an arm over her shoulder.

"The pond's gonna be nice, yeah?"

Kate shrugged his arm away playfully and started down the path.

"Ice cold, remember?" she called over her shoulder.

Connor mumbled something about *somebody* being ice cold, and put one arm on Ben's shoulder and the other on Alex's—Connor's standard position as king of the boys. Alex wore an olive green fanny pack I hadn't seen before.

"Provisions?" I asked, eyeing the pack.

"I wish," Alex said, touching the pouch strapped to

his side with a black belt. "Turns out I've got some kind of wacky diabetes/low blood sugar thing going on. It's complicated. Insulin shots in here, just in case."

"Sorry to hear that," Ben said. "Does it hurt?"

Alex unzipped the pack and took out a container holding three syringes of clear fluid. "I've only had to use it twice, but yeah, it hurts like a mother. Kind of hot going in."

"Bummer," said Ben, and Alex put the packet of needles away as we kept walking.

Marisa fell into step with me at the back of the line and started singing *I wanna be adored* in a sleepy, singsong voice.

"Like old times," Connor yelled back, then howled at the sky like we were heading through a tunnel at the start of a football game.

I remembered how I'd felt a year before when I'd started down this path for the first time. Before I'd been cured, I was terrified of these people. All I could think about was getting away and hiding in the woods.

"You're not going to run off on us, are you, Will?" Alex called back, laughing it up with the other guys. It was like he'd read my mind.

"Not on my watch," Kate said. "We're done by nightfall

or I'm driving away without you guys. I don't have a lot of interest in being stuck out here after dark."

"Ditto," said Ben.

"Are you hearing this?" Marisa, leaning in close, whispered the words. I nodded yes and, looking at them, wondered how I'd ever been afraid of these people.

The crows were still hanging around in the trees, chasing us down the path like the first time we'd come this way. When we reached the fork on the trail, I remembered how I'd turned off, leaving the group behind, dead set on going it alone.

"Feels spooky down here," said Alex, but he was far enough up front that I barely heard him. Connor let out a huge *boo!* and Ben told him to shut up.

It was cooler down there, and darker under the canopy of trees. Sunlight trickled through in fiery splotches at our feet.

Everyone stopped ahead of us and I pulled up a little short, suddenly unsure about what we were all doing. We were miles from anywhere, and I was the only one who knew how dangerous it really was. I looked at Marisa and felt a wave of regret for having brought her back— for having brought all of them back—to the place where they were cured of their fears. They had no memory of the things that had been done to them. But I knew.

I knew, and still I'd brought them here.

I would soon regret that decision.

"There she is," said Connor, lolling back and forth like the walk down had taken a lot out of him. "Same as before."

I crept closer and saw what he was talking about. The looming concrete-slab walls covered in moss and ivy, still looking more like a giant coffin than a building.

Fort Eden.

"God, it's so creepy looking," said Kate. She was rattled, which was saying something. "How'd we ever get the nerve up to go in there the first time?"

Ben Dugan went so far as to back up and bump into me before stopping cold.

"This is starting to feel like a bad idea," he said. "Why the hell are we even here?"

"Because Mrs. Goring wants to see us," I said.

"What about Rainsford? Is he here, too?" Ben asked.

This was the tough part. There was a huge secret about Rainsford only I among the group knew. I hadn't even told Marisa.

"Let's get it over with," Connor said, manning up as he always did. "I'm hungry. Maybe she's got some Mrs.

Goring Spaghetti in there waiting for us."

Connor started into the clearing, then looked back at us like we were a bunch of lowly players required to follow him. Kate rolled her eyes but trudged off, giving in to the inevitable, and that started an exodus from the foot of the trail to the entrance of the fort.

The guys took turns knocking on the locked door, but no one answered.

"Where'd she say she'd be?" asked Alex. He was settling into the adventure even as he kept looking around like someone was watching us.

I shrugged, I didn't know. Everyone was staring at me like I was insane.

"Maybe we should leave," I suggested. It felt like there was still a chance to get everyone out safely before Mrs. Goring showed up with a shotgun and guided us all into a fear chamber in the basement of the concrete building. My mind was starting to fill with bad possibilities.

Kate laughed unkindly and started marching for the second of two structures on the property,[1] the Bunker. "You talked us into this, Will. This was *your* thing, not ours."

---

[1] I have recordings of all the cures that took place at Fort Eden the last time we were there. I've posted them at www.willbesting.com. To see Kate's cure and understand a little more about why she is plagued by terrible headaches, visit the site and use the password *hollander*.

She rubbed her temples as she stormed off, and I felt sad for her. The headaches hadn't stopped. They probably never would.

Marisa followed after Kate, but all four of us guys stayed put. It felt like we weren't really being invited to go knock on the Bunker door, like we better stay right where we were and keep our mouths shut.

"Dang, Will. What were you thinking?" said Connor. "Dragging us all the way out here for what?"

"Yeah, what gives?" asked Alex.

Ben just stared off into the woods like he wished he was home.

"All I know is I got a letter and it said she'd be here. It said she was sick or dying or something. She wanted to see us, that's it. End of story."

They already knew everything I was saying, I'd told them about ten times each. But it didn't matter. We'd spent half the day getting down here, and the place was looking deserted as Kate and Marisa came back.

"Nobody home," said Marisa.

"Unless she's already dead."

Kate had said the thing I was wondering, and looking at the faces staring back at me, it seemed like everyone else was thinking the same thing, too.

"No way I'm climbing through some window looking for a dead body," said Ben. "Forget it. I'm outta here."

He started walking away, but Connor grabbed him by the arm.

"Let's at least jump in the pond while we're down here. It'll take like ten minutes."

More likely Connor was thinking about how much work it would be hiking out of the ravine and back to the cars and hoped for a little more time to rest. His dizzy spells were always a lot worse when he exerted himself.[2]

"It might feel good to get wet before we go," said Marisa, smiling awkwardly at the group. "It is hot out here."

"And it's a hell of a hike out," Connor added, which seemed to bring everyone halfheartedly into alignment with the idea of cooling off first.

It was agreed we'd forgo searching for a dead version of Mrs. Goring and dare each other to leap into the freezing pond instead. This seemed to chipper everyone up the farther we got away from Fort Eden on a grassy path in the woods. I remembered my first walk with Marisa down the same trail and felt a swell of emotion, taking her hand as she leaned into me.

---

[2] Connor's cure left him with an ailment that sidelined him from sports for good. He was bitter about it and still believed he'd be playing again soon, once the doctors figured out what was going on. To see his cure, use the password *falling* at www.willbesting.com.

"I remember, too," she whispered, close and warm.

I don't know why it hadn't occurred to me before, but something struck me then as I looked above and saw a crow staring angrily down at me.

This whole situation could have gone terribly wrong.

I might have had to tell them the truth.

What had I been thinking, dragging them all out here in the first place?

No sooner had I processed this thought and squeezed Marisa's hand tighter, than I noticed everyone had turned in my direction on the path. They'd arrived at the clearing before the pond and stopped short, still and quiet, as if a rare creature was up ahead and they might scare it off.

It was certainly rare, what they saw, but it was no wild animal.

As I stepped past Connor and Kate and the rest, my eyes settled on a figure standing at the dock. She was staring out over the still, glassy water, her shock of hair a brilliant white in the sunlight.

Mrs. Goring was not dead after all.

She turned to us without smiling; her dark eyes the only moving things against the granite stillness of her face. At length, Mrs. Goring moved a few steps closer.

"My god you're loud," she said unapologetically, as if it was our fault we hadn't searched where she was standing sooner. "Like a herd of elephants."

Mrs. Goring's gaze landed on me, and I felt the full force of her will like a blast of hot wind in my face. She was searching my expression, trying to read my thoughts.

You didn't tell them, did you? Not even Marisa.

No, Mrs. Goring, I didn't tell them. Not even Marisa. It's not exactly easy stuff to tell if you don't have to.

Mrs. Goring lost interest in staring at my face as she walked toward us. She wore the same clumsy boots, half tied, with the heavy heels clubbing the dock with each step; the same flannel shirt even in the blistering heat. And she was annoyed at our presence, like we'd invaded her privacy.

"I told Cynthia to have you here *early*," she continued. "It's noon."

Nobody answered, but everyone else had to be thinking the same thing I was: *you invited us up here. We drove two hours and hiked down into a ravine on the hottest day of the summer. Nice to see you, too.*

But no one was about to say what they really felt, not even Kate or Connor. Mrs. Goring had that effect on people.

"Let me take a wild guess. You haven't eaten since

breakfast and now you expect me to feed you."

Connor started to open his mouth, but Marisa cut him off.

"We're fine. You don't need to cook for us. We just came to say hi and see how you were doing."

"Sure you did," Mrs. Goring snapped, and I wished I'd had the courage to tell her to shut up and leave Marisa alone. But I didn't.

"There are things I need to tell you, and quick," she went on, pointing her chin toward me. "Me and him, we both have *information*, don't we, Will Besting?"

She said it like she was almost enjoying the fact that I'd withheld certain important facts she and I both knew. She had been right about me, or so she thought.

I was a coward.

Mrs. Goring took one more look at us and let out a large, impatient sigh.

"Come on, I've got pancakes and a jar of peanut butter at the Bunker. That's all you're getting."

She moved toward us, and we broke apart like crepe paper so she didn't have to slow down. She was fast, four or five steps away before any of us tacitly agreed to eat her food by marching in line behind her.

"I didn't think you'd all come," she said, turning and staring at Ben Dugan without stopping. "Especially him."

Ben didn't take the implication that he was weak or spineless without firing back.

"You walk pretty fast for someone who's supposed to be on her deathbed."

Mrs. Goring cackled, sending a crow flying off a nearby branch, screeching back at her.

"We're all dying, Ben Dugan. Some of us a lot faster than others."

No one else tried going toe to toe with Mrs. Goring after that, and a heavy silence fell among us. When we reached the fort, Mrs. Goring unlocked the door, pushing it open.

"You know the drill. Wait at the table, I'll bring the pancakes."

She started to walk away as we gathered like a flock of birds at the foot of the stairs leading up to the door. As I stared off toward her makeshift house I thought I saw a figure move near the front window. But the wind was blowing through the trees, casting long shadows over the Bunker and Fort Eden, playing tricks with my eyes.

"If you're not dying, then why are we here?" Kate asked Mrs. Goring. She had a genuine look of curiosity on her face as Mrs. Goring stared coldly at me.

"Ask him," she said, and then she was moving toward

the Bunker, the only other building on the property.

Everyone stared at me, and I felt the weight of my Recorder in my back pocket.

I knew there was something on the device I should have shown them before we left. I'd thought maybe Mrs. Goring really was dying, that my secret could stay hidden.

But I had been wrong.

Looking at Marisa and knowing what this might do to us, I wished Mrs. Goring would drop dead right there in the woods.

=== ===

"It's my Recorder," I said. "I record things with it."[3]

I sounded about as dumb as I looked, but it didn't change the fact that I was making everyone nervous.

"What kinds of things have you recorded?" asked

---

[3] When I'd turned twelve, my mom introduced me to online college classes at a tech school in India. They were cheap courses taught by thickly accented Indian tech gods about stuff I actually had some interest in. First I took video game programming, then a series on electronics, then hardware integration. I failed approximately half of the classes I took, but my interest was sparked.

I was an audio geek at heart, but I liked video, too. Homebrew degrees in electronics and programming pushed me over the edge. I ended up on craigslist buying up old iPods and digital cameras until my money ran out.

Then I opened them up and started digging around.

Sure, my Recorder was basically the same thing as a new iPhone without the phone part; but I'd built it myself, and it looked gnarly.

Alex. He'd been fairly aloof up until then, but sitting around the table in a tight circle with the rest of us he was suddenly alert.

I pushed a button on my Recorder, a device that had the look and feel of a first-generation digital music player.

"I just recorded you talking, so there's that."

"And it records video, too. Right, Will?" Marisa said. She knew all about it, just not all the stuff that was hidden inside, buried behind passwords.

"Why do I get the feeling you've got recordings of me on there?" asked Kate. It wasn't so much a question as a statement: *if you did that, I'm going to tell Connor to kick your ass.*

"Look, you guys . . ." I was getting an old familiar feeling of wanting to be alone. Under the table I took Marisa's hand, partly because it was a comfort, but also because I had a bad feeling it might be the last time I'd ever get to do it. Mrs. Goring was going to be back any minute. I was cornered, trapped, unprepared.

Better I tell them than have Mrs. Goring do the dirty work for me. It would only be worse.

"Just tell us, Will," said Marisa, squeezing my hand. "It can't be that bad."

Oh yes it can, I thought.

"Before I came here, before we all came here," I began, glancing between all the eyes staring back at me curiously. "I was afraid to be near anyone. You guys know that, right? You know I couldn't come in here. I was a different person back then."

This was all true. I'd had an acute fear—we'd all had one.

The fears were these:

> Will Besting (that was me): Fear of being
> with people my own age
> Marisa Sorrento: Fear of being kidnapped
> Ben Dugan: Fear of bugs, spiders, centipedes
> Kate Hollander: Fear of doctors, hospitals,
> clinics
> Alex Hersh: Fear of dogs
> Conner Bloom: Fear of falling
> Avery Varone: Fear of death

And everyone had been cured. *Totally* cured, the fears wiped away entirely.

But there had been a cost, something I knew that they didn't.

I repeated what I'd said, looking back at them as they sat there trying to figure out where this was all going.

"I was different back then. I'm not that person anymore."

"None of us are the same as we were before we came

here, Will," said Ben, and I felt like he was trying to understand. "Why does that matter?"

"If you had been like me, wouldn't you have wanted to know?"

"Know what?" asked Ben.

"If you were afraid of being around a lot of people, wouldn't you have done everything you could to know what you were getting yourself into?"

"God, Will, just spill it already." Kate was running low on patience as she popped two Tylenol in her mouth and choked them down with no water.

"I know what Will is trying to tell you," Marisa said. She had moved her hand to my forearm, gripping it tightly like she, too, was about to be on the wrong side of the group.

"No, Marisa, it's more than that," I said, staring into her eyes as my own started to pool with fear. My voice was shaking when I told them the first of what I needed to say.

"I knew about you all. Before this place. I knew."

It was not the revelation that would ruin everything. No, that part would be much worse.

They stared back at me, unsure of what I meant, so I went on.

"We all had the same doctor—"

"Wait a second," said Kate, leaning forward with her sharp elbows on the table. She had a kind of beauty that was at its most powerful when she was furious. Connor and Ben couldn't take their eyes off her. "Are you telling us you took that *thing* in there and recorded our sessions?"

"Like with a remote control from the sidewalk or what?" asked Alex, who seemed thoroughly confused.

I explained what I'd really done, which unfortunately sounded a little bit worse than what Kate had guessed.

"Dr. Stevens recorded all of us, every session. I just figured out the password on her computer and uploaded them all to my Recorder."

"Harsh," said Ben. He wouldn't look me in the eye. "So you listened to all my private sessions?"

"No, only a few."

"Face it, you're not that interesting, bro," said Connor, which loosened everyone up at least a little. But what he said next made me his fan for life. "Come on, you guys, be real. If you'd have thought of it and had the guts to do it and had the brains to pull it off, you'd have done the same thing."

Everyone sort of looked at the table, even Kate seemed

to lose some of her steam as her attractiveness scaled back from an 11 out of 10 to a 9.7.

"And I for one am glad Will has that stuff," said Marisa, coming to my defense for what I was sure would be the last time ever. "Dr. Stevens wouldn't have given those files to us. Now we can get them from Will if we ever want to go back and remember what freaks we all were."

There was nervous laughter as she stared up at me with those endlessly deep brown eyes, and I knew what she was feeling: proud. Proud that I'd told my secret.

Now to obliterate all hope of ever having a girlfriend again.

"There's more," I said, and even then, *right* then, I saw something in Marisa's eyes change.

Wait, what do you mean, more? What didn't you tell me?

Oh, nothing much, only a secret the size of Texas, I thought.

"Come on, Will, get it all out," said Connor, who seemed to think anything from the past was fair game, harmless, not a huge deal. I was starting to see that this was really what it was all about for him: making a mole-hill out of a mountain. If he downplayed the situation, none of it would mean anything.

Sorry, Connor. No one would be happier than me if that were true.

I was just about to spill the beans when the side door leading down to the Bunker basement flew open and a metal cart rolled into the room. A flash of memories washed over me at the sound of the wobbly wheel on the cart as she pushed it toward us.

The bomb shelter, the monitors, the cures.

The hypnotic, whispering voice of Rainsford.

Keith, my dead brother, in his lime green baseball cap.

That son of a bitch Davis and his flash of teeth when he smiled.

Avery. Where was Avery?

"Move it or lose it!" Mrs. Goring screamed as she shoved the cart toward us. Ben and Alex had to push back in their chairs in order to miss being clobbered, and the cart bashed against the table, upsetting a plastic jar of peanut butter that rolled off the cart and onto the floor.

"Someone pick that up," Mrs. Goring said. "And plug this in. I assume Mr. Besting has failed to get to the point and it will be up to me."

There were several things on the cart besides the empty space where the jar of peanut butter had been

31

Airdrie Public Library

(a jar I was more than happy to go in search of so the attention would be off me for a few seconds). On the cart sat seven or eight gigantic pancakes stacked on a single plate, a small pile of butter knives, and a computer monitor. The monitor was attached to a dusty old computer sitting on the bottom shelf of the cart, from which a cord dangled like a tail.

"You," she said, pointing at me as I returned to my seat, peanut butter jar in hand. "Plug this stupid thing in. You had your chance."

Part of me was incredibly bummed out by this turn of events, but another part was glad not to have to do the deed myself. This way, I could blame it on her. She'd made me stay quiet against my will. As I plugged in the computer and listened to it whirl to life, I put this plan into play.

Whatever she tells them, just remember: she made me keep it secret.

Mrs. Goring picked up the plate of Frisbee-size pancakes and dropped it with a crash on the table. She grabbed all the butter knives with one hand and sort of punched Ben Dugan in the shoulder with her balled-up fist of metal. He took this to mean he should pass out the knives and began doing so.

She gazed at Marisa long and hard. "You knew he was a coward when you kissed him. Don't act so surprised."

The only person brave enough or hungry enough to actually start pasting peanut butter on a giant cold pancake was Connor Bloom. The rest of us just sat there staring as the monitor flashed to life, first with a pale green sort of light, then more brightly with a bluish twang of fuzz. Mrs. Goring began fumbling with the keys on the computer keyboard, looking at the monitor like she was staring into a fogged mirror trying to make out her own face.

"If you haven't taken a pancake by the time I start this show, you won't get one," she said, not looking at anyone. "And it may be a while before you eat again."

What was that supposed to mean? I thought as I watched every single person take a floppy pancake off the plate. I picked one up, too. It felt like something cold and dead draped across my hand.

"I will not go into detail," said Mrs. Goring, picking up the plate just as Connor stole the last one (also his second). "I will tell you only two things, nothing more. If you want details beyond that, you'll have to ask him. He knows everything, even if he tells you he doesn't."

Her cold gaze didn't move from my face during

everything she said, which felt like an anvil resting on top of any resolve I might have had to defend myself. I was powerless against this fierce little woman with her boots and her white hair.

"The first is this," she said, and my heart dropped into my stomach. I tore a piece of the pancake off and shoved it in my mouth so I'd have something else to do besides freak out. Marisa's hand lay soft in my own, not holding mine, not yet pulling away. "You all have ailments you didn't possess when you got here. You know you have them and you know they're getting worse."

"My parents are suing Dr. Stevens about that," said Alex. "Only they can't find her."

"Shut up! One more word and I take the pancake."

Sometimes Mrs. Goring was amusing despite herself.

"You've all taken on one element of *his*. You're not hurt or sick. Not really. You're just old, as he was once old."

Connor leaned over next to me and whispered, "What the hell is she talking about?"

"Give it," she said, holding out her hand, and even Connor didn't have the guts to say no. He handed over one of his two pancakes.

"Rainsford, the person who cured you," Mrs. Goring

went on, dropping the heavy pancake onto the cart. "He also stole something from you. He stole your youth. Not all of it, just a piece of it. And what he left behind in your body are the ailments you now endure. Will! Can you hear me, Will?"

I could, but not that well. My hearing was halfway shot.

"You're crazy, you know that?" Kate went on, emboldened by a new idea: maybe Mrs. Goring was insane. "What does that even mean? He made us old?"

"You think I'm nuts?" asked Mrs. Goring, and then, looking at me, "Ask him. Am I crazy, Will Besting? *Am I!?*"

I didn't speak. I couldn't. And in that moment Mrs. Goring pressed her finger to the keyboard and the screen for the oldest computer I'd seen in a long time began to play a video I'd witnessed many, many times. Hundreds of times. It was on my Recorder. I'd watched it in bed, over and over again, trying to understand.

The video showed Rainsford, the old and sinister man who had cured us of our fears. It was his face in close-up as he stared back at the camera, a face that began to twitch and move, to convulse. And then it began to change. The skin tightened and the face filled with life.

The man grew younger before our eyes until finally, with alarming finality, it was clear who he was.[4]

"Davis?" Ben Dugan muttered.

Mrs. Goring didn't speak, she simply stood erect, gauging the expressions on our faces. Davis, who had acted like our friend and our helper. It was Rainsford all along. The two people were one and the same.

"Let me get this straight," said Alex, scratching the side of his face like he actually had any kind of stubble at all, which he did not. "You're telling us that Rainsford, the guy that cured us, was taking something from us that made him young again?"

"That's what I'm telling you," said Mrs. Goring. "It's what he does. There is no more Rainsford. Now there is only Davis, at least for another fifty years or so. Then he'll do it again. And again. And again!"

"The Dude is a vampire," said Connor. "That's twisted."

But even in his attempt to ease the fear around us, he glared at me.

They were all glaring at me.

"You *knew* this?" Marisa asked me, her hand slipping away. "But how? How did you know?"

[4] To watch Rainsford transform, go to www.willbesting.com and use the password *transformation*.

I shook my head.

"I knew because she told me everything," I finally managed. "And because I didn't listen to Rainsford. I wasn't in there with you guys. I didn't listen, so he couldn't make me forget."

Mrs. Goring's first name was Eve, and like the biblical Eve, she had stripped them of their innocence, opening their minds to the truth and blowing my world apart in the process.

Marisa's warm, soft hand slipped completely away from mine, and I knew everything had suddenly changed.

She'd stopped trusting me.

———

It took some convincing.

Mrs. Goring had to tell more than she wanted to and so did I, but finally, a half hour later, all the pancakes but one were gone and everyone believed. Old Rainsford had become young Davis. He had taken something from each of us in order to make that happen. He had figured out a way to become young again at our expense.

Mrs. Goring picked up the one remaining pancake

and took a bite out of it; then she spoke with her mouth full.

"What creature in the morning goes on four legs, at midday on two, and in the evening on three, and the more legs it has, the weaker it be?"

Kate was in no mood for riddles as she pushed away from the table and stood up.

"I'm leaving. Who's with me?"

"Sit down," said Mrs. Goring. Her words were slow, measured, and powerful—but not powerful enough to stop Kate Hollander.

"News flash! You can't make me stay here. You can't make *any* of us stay."

Alex got up, too. Then Marisa and Connor. This potential mass exodus rattled Mrs. Goring as she looked at me for help.

"Sorry, Mrs. Goring, *I* don't even know why we're here," I said, and it was true.

Mrs. Goring watched as Ben Dugan also got up and the whole procession began moving for the door. It was only me at the table, alone. I stared at the empty chairs around me and answered Mrs. Goring's question.

"It's man," I said, which was a strange enough thing to say that it got Kate to turn on her heels and glare at me.

"You're as loony as she is."

"I'm just looking for answers. Don't you want some answers, Kate?"

"Yeah, I want answers. Ones that make sense!" Kate started moving back toward me, her enraged splendor in full bloom. "*It's man?* You're a freak, Will. A total freak."

"All I know is I have at least one answer right."

Mrs. Goring repeated the riddle.

"What creature in the morning goes on four legs, at midday on two, and in the evening on three, and the more legs it has, the weaker it be?"

"Man?" Connor said, as he and the gang slowly walked back toward the table. "How is it man? I don't get it."

"It's the riddle of the sphinx," I said. "It's mythology."

"Hey, I remember that!" Ben was back at the table, bolstered with memory. "We went through the whole thing in eighth grade. He's right, it's man. We start on four legs, you know, like babies crawling around on the floor. Then we stand up and walk until we get old. Then we get a cane to help us walk, that's the three legs."

"Then we die," Marisa concluded. She'd returned to the table, too, but she was no longer next to me.

"Unless you're Rainsford," said Mrs. Goring, a sad

sort of rage in her voice. "If you're him, you never die. You just stay on two legs forever, walking on all the dead people you leave behind. Laughing."

Mrs. Goring did sound crazy as a loon, and maybe she was. But she had our attention.

"Why are we here?" asked Kate. She was confused and annoyed, but she was also curious.

"What if I told you I could get back what's been taken from you?"

That caught everyone's interest, including mine. She looked at Connor Bloom.

"What if you could stop having those dizzy spells? You could be the captain of the football team again. And you," she turned her gaze on Marisa, pausing to stare deep into her eyes. "You want to take a long nap right now, don't you? Wouldn't it be nice to stop seeing the world as a disconnected haze?"

Marisa couldn't hold her stare as Mrs. Goring silently slipped her hand into a pocket and took out a glass vial of liquid. Whatever was trapped inside was black. She pointed the end in our direction, and we saw that it was the kind of glass container used for holding a blood sample.

"Gross," said Alex. "You're carrying blood around in your pocket?"

"Shut up, Alex." Connor had sat back down—they all had—and he was leaning forward on his elbows, looking seriously at the vial. If there was a shred of hope he might be restored to his former glory, he wanted to know every detail.

"This is not just any blood," Mrs. Goring answered. "It's my own, and something more."

She held it up to the light, sloshing its contents back and forth, and I got the sense that what was inside was thicker than blood. It looked like old motor oil.

"You're not the only ones who've been cured," she said. "A long time ago, before any of you were a bad idea in the minds of your dim-witted parents, he cured me, too."

"No way," said Ben. "Were you two like, you know, together?"

"We really don't need to hear about this," said Alex, obviously grossed out by the idea of Mrs. Goring and Rainsford disrobing each other.

"One of you is missing," Mrs. Goring said, ignoring both boys. "Avery. She's the new me, you see? He's taken her for his own, at least for a while. But time will pass, and when it does, she will grow old. They both will."

"But he'll do this to seven more people like us," said

Kate. "Is that what you're telling us? And Avery will end up just like you: old and bitter and alone."

"And here I was actually starting to like you," said Mrs. Goring. "You should learn to tame that wild tongue of yours."

Kate had gotten under Mrs. Goring's skin and put her in an even worse mood. Perfect.

"Tell me what you were going to say," said Connor. He'd been wobbling back and forth a little bit, having one of his spells, but he was back now. "About getting back what he took from me."

Mrs. Goring observed Connor with a contemptible pity, and it seemed she was having a hard time deciding whether to answer his plea or continue fighting with Kate. The negative energy in the room suited her, a long-missing fuel pumping into her hollowed-out soul.

"This vial is filled with my fear," she said, pointing the tube violently in Kate's direction, while answering Connor's question. "It's the essence of what passed between me and Rainsford, or more accurately, the sludge created out of the cure. I've carried it around a long time. Avery carries hers, too. It's our burden to carry the curse of young love around in our pockets so we never forget what fools we were."

She turned her head slightly and stared at Connor. "But your fear is somewhere else. Your vial is hidden away in a secret place."

"What about mine?" Alex prodded.

Mrs. Goring snapped her attention to Alex, then Ben, then me, and finally Marisa.

"All of your fears are hidden away. But I know where he keeps them. And if you bring them to me, I can give back what he took from you."

"You mean no more pain in my hands and my back?" Ben asked, who suffered daily from debilitating arthritis. "That problem would go away?"

"Yes, that would go away. You'd still be stupid, but the pain—that I can fix."

Kate laughed and turned to Connor, expecting him to join her, but he was all business.

"Where do we sign up?"

Commanding an army of shoulder-padded Neanderthals across the goal line again made up the sum total of his dreams.

"I would need them all," she stammered. It seemed to me she was surprised to have gotten to this stage so easily. She had underestimated Connor's will to compete.

"God, this is twisted," said Kate. "What would you even do if you had them?"

At this, Mrs. Goring offered a fleeting smile that lasted only a moment.

"I can't get back what he stole from me. I'm cursed to hold the rank of seven, like Avery, and we are among the few who can never go back. But you I can help. Your wretched blood can be your antidote."

"You'd insert our blood back into us?" asked Ben. "That doesn't sound like such a good idea."

"All of your vials together, that's the antidote."

"Whoa, hold on," said Kate. "You mean we go find these things—these vials of whatever—then you make some sort of witch's brew and stick a needle in my arm?"

"And then I pump you full of blood from this bunch of idiots," said Mrs. Goring, leaning over the table and staring down at Kate Hollander. "Yes, that's the cure."

There was a certain logic to it, in a black magic sort of way, that somewhere within all our mire lay a cure for what ailed us. But I didn't trust her just the same.

"How do you know it will work?" I asked. "And why should we believe you?"

"I know because he told me. And you should trust me because I hate him just as much as you do. We're bound by our loathing of the same person. And besides, the same thing that will cure you? It will *kill* him. That's my take in the bargain. You get cured, I get a way to put an end to this madness, an end to Rainsford, once and for all."

"A poison for the one guy who can't be killed," Alex commented. "Interesting."

"But he's gone," I said, feeling inside that I'd love to be the one to stick the needle into his arm. "You don't even know where he is."

"I'm banking on his return at some point in the not-too-distant future. He's careful about cleaning up his messes, and you, Will Besting, are a mess."

I pondered what that meant as Mrs. Goring stood stone cold, with her arms folded over her chest. She'd said her piece, but there was one thing she hadn't told us. I was thinking about the one thing, but it was Marisa with her haunted, weary voice who asked.

"What was your fear?"

Mrs. Goring put the vial back in her pocket.

"I am the anti-Will Besting. Or I was."

"You were afraid of being alone?" I asked, surprised by the revelation.

"Not anymore, as you can plainly see by my circumstances. I've come to understand that people are nothing but trouble and silence is golden."

"If you're lying to us," said Kate, standing in unison with the rest of us as Mrs. Goring started for the door, "I'll kill you."

Mrs. Goring didn't bother to respond as she walked the length of Fort Eden and put her hand on the handle of the door.

"It's time to take back what's yours," she said without turning back.

And then she was out the door and we were all following her.

———

On the way to the pond, there was a flurry of questions about where we were going and what we would be required to do, accompanied by a grand total of zero answers from the woman in charge. Mrs. Goring had fallen into an impenetrable silence. It was a lonely walk, because no one would look at me. I'd betrayed them, Marisa most of all, and they weren't going to let me forget it.

Keith, little bro, I wish you were here.

Don't sweat it. They're just a bunch of losers. You don't need them.

What about Marisa?

It's not like you were gonna marry her. Grow up.

Sometimes the conversations I have with my dead brother are not as useful as I hope they will be. As I was lost in my pretend Keith world, I looked back toward Fort Eden. The wind was still moving through the tall trees along the path, casting those sharp shadows on the ground, but this time it wasn't a shadow I saw moving behind me. I'd caught a glimpse of someone moving from one side of the woods to the other. I dropped back from the rest of the group without being noticed. If anything, they *wanted* to leave me behind like the first time we'd been here. They wished I didn't exist, and that made it easier to be invisible.

I didn't have to drop back very far before darting into the woods at the edge of the narrow, winding path. They'd only assume I was falling behind as usual and leave me be, at least that's what I thought as I quickly doubled back on the side where I was sure I'd seen someone. I fought through underbrush and worked my way around a series of tall trees, but there was no one.

What I wouldn't give to be able to hear a little better, I thought. If only I could listen for someone walking or running away, I'd know where to go. I was about to run back and catch up to the others before they realized I was gone, and that's when I saw it, caught on a sharp limb of a tree. I edged closer, peering in every direction for signs of life, and grabbed what I'd found.

I held it tightly in my hand as I jumped back onto the path and double-timed it around two twisting corners, seeing the group up ahead. They were slowing down as I came in close, looking back at me like I'd been there all along.

I stuffed what I'd found into my front pocket before anyone else could see it.

As my fingers felt the softness of the item, it made me feel even surer that something wasn't right at Fort Eden.

It was scary, this thing I'd found, for one very important reason.

It proved that we were not alone.

Someone else was hiding out at Fort Eden.

———

"Any of you ever been in the pump house?" Mrs. Goring asked, breaking her silence as we came to the dock.

No one raised a hand as Connor leaned down and splashed water on his face, but all eyes were on the run-down wooden structure that sat next to the pond. It was small, like the gardening shed in my backyard at home, and it looked like it might not make it through a hard winter.

"It's not really a pump house," Mrs. Goring continued. Then she walked away in the direction of the thing we were talking about and left us all scratching our heads about what was really inside.

She took a ring of keys out of her pocket and went to work on a big padlock at the door while Alex joked lamely about how easy it would be to put his foot through one of the walls and walk right in. When the heavy lock was removed, Mrs. Goring flung the door open and stood aside.

"When you get to the bottom, you'll find a room. Your vials are stored in there with all the others."

"The *others*? Wait—what *others*?" Kate asked.

"He's been at this a long time, or did I neglect to mention that?"

Ben Dugan peered inside the dark, damp space, and when he talked his voice had a soft echo. "How old is Rainsford, really?"

Mrs. Goring wouldn't say, but I thought I had an answer.

"Seven vials for every time he went from old to young, only the seventh person keeps theirs on them. So all we have to do is divide the number of vials we find by six. If there are sixty vials down there, he's ten times seventy. He'd be seven hundred years old."

"Are we getting this done or doing algebra?" Connor complained. "If there are a bunch of vials down there, how will we know which ones are ours?"

"You'll know," said Mrs. Goring impatiently. "Trust me, it will be obvious."

"And why don't you just get them yourself?" Alex suggested.

"The way down isn't for someone old like me, and the door is too heavy at the bottom. I can't open it."

"Why do we all have to go down there?" asked Ben. "Why not just Will? He got us into this mess."

"Did not," I said. Getting dumped on was growing old fast. "We all got cured, we all got symptoms. How is any of that my fault?"

"I think we should all go," Connor said, "Come on, it'll be cool." And that, more than anything, is probably what got us to do it. In the end it was like a dare no one wanted to miss out on. And there was the promise of a cure, even if the promise was made by an insane woman living all alone in the woods. It was something to hold on to.

"At least make him go first," Alex said. "That way if I fall I'll land on his head."

Marisa didn't come to my defense. She wouldn't even look at me. It got worse when Connor started whispering to her, glancing over his shoulder as I fumed.

She's back on the market. Nice. That's what his muscle-headed look told me, and Marisa didn't do anything to make him think otherwise.

"Fine, I'll go first," I said, blowing past everyone and arriving inside, where a metal door with a latch sat against the ground. Mrs. Goring knelt down beside me and grabbed the lever with her hand, shoving it sideways with a grinding noise that reverberated into places I couldn't see.

"He's older," Mrs. Goring whispered close to my ear, and I turned to her. "Let's make sure he doesn't see one more bloody year."

She shoved something in my hand and looked at me as if it was to remain our secret, whatever it was. Did I really think it was a good idea to conspire with Mrs. Goring again? She'd gotten me in a heap of trouble with Marisa and the rest, and yet I had a weird feeling I should let it pass. It crossed my mind to tell her about what I'd found in the woods, but there was no time.

"Agreed," I said, staring down a long, wide tube with a metal ladder on one side. There was faint, crackling light coming from somewhere far below. I slid what she'd handed me into my back pocket and listened carefully for any sound coming from the depths of whatever lay belowground at Fort Eden.

"Good thing you're not afraid of heights, Connor," I said, imagining the old Connor Bloom, the one who had been terrified of falling.[5]

I started down the ladder, feeling the rungs grow colder as I went, and immediately decided it was a bad idea. I stopped and started to complain, to reason with the others that we should go back, but Connor was the second one into the tube and he wouldn't stop coming toward me. His body was a hulking shadow against the light of the world outside.

"Go, man! I don't want to be down here all day."

I didn't move. I could feel the stupidity of what we were doing. It suddenly felt all wrong, just in time to have no power over what was happening to me.

---

[5] To see Connor's cure and experience his fear firsthand, go to my site, www.willbesting.com, and use the password *falling*.

"I'm going to step on your hand," said Connor. He was staring down at me from above with a resolve that bordered on psychotic. "I'm getting those vials, and you're going to help me do it. Move."

He placed one shoe on my left hand and began pressing down with his weight. Looking down, I saw that it was at least thirty feet more to the bottom.

"Okay, okay!" I shouted. "Back off!"

Connor removed his foot and I reluctantly went down another four rungs as someone else came in behind Connor, I couldn't tell who.

If I could just keep Marisa out of here. At least that would be something, I thought. But I kept on, Connor's relentless feet at my head, until I stood on a slick concrete floor and stared up. I could see all of them marching down the ladder in a line like little soldiers.

And at the very top, Mrs. Goring's head, which suddenly disappeared.

And that's when the metal door at the top of the ladder slammed shut, before half of us were even off the ladder.

I heard the handle turn way up there, grinding into the locked position, so it had to be loud. When everyone made it to the bottom, no one wanted to say what was really going on. We just stood there, still and quiet, and tried to come to grips with the reality of our circumstances.

We'd driven two hours out of L.A., walked down a very long and steep path into a desolate wood known by only a few. We'd trusted a crazy woman and let her lead us a hundred feet underground.

And we'd let her close the door on us.

We were trapped.

3:00 PM — 4:00 PM

3:00 PM—3:30 PM

"It's locked, and it's unbelievably dark up there."

Alex was back, sitting on the floor like he'd run a marathon, complaining about how much pain he was in. He put his hand on that olive green fanny pack at his side, and I could tell he was thinking about sticking himself with one of the needles. We might have sent the wrong guy, given his circulation problems. He'd climbed all the way to the top and tested the door, just to make 100 percent certain that a lunatic had just locked us underground.

"So we've got an insane witch holding us captive in the woods," Kate said, shaking her head. "I didn't wake up this morning thinking this was possible, but hanging out with you guys again, it's starting to feel like it was inevitable."

While Alex[6] had been climbing all the way up and back down the ladder, the rest of us had waited, too nervous to fan out or go very far from the entryway before knowing for sure what we'd gotten ourselves into. The biggest reason for the holdup, I think, was what the place looked like. Three hallways led off in different directions, each with a different-colored arrow on the floor and a sparse set of words:

RED ZONE

BLUE ZONE / O ZONE

GREEN ZONE

But it was the shape and quality of the passageways that bothered me the most. When I was a kid, there was a round culvert that ran under a road near my house. It

---

[6] Alex was the third guy to get cured at Ford Eden. He was afraid of dogs because of an incident when he was a kid. If you want to see his cure, I posted it. After the cure his legs kept going to sleep on him, you know, like when you wake up and you can't feel your big toe and when it comes back it's needles and pins? Like that. It's like he's sixteen, but his circulation is seventy years old. Check it: www.willbesting.com, password *throwmeabone*.

was big enough to crawl down the center of and end up on the other side, but there came a time when I wouldn't do that anymore because it made me feel claustrophobic. There were a lot of bugs in there, plus I started thinking there might be a possum or a family of rats making a home out of it. The passageways under Fort Eden were like that, only a lot bigger. They were circular tubes, about fifteen feet around, with ridged edges like a Ruffles potato chip. They were also rusted out and gnarly looking, like acid and rotten water had chewed away at the integrity of the metal for a hundred years.

They were lit with yellow lightbulbs that were crackling on and off with life or dimmed to near uselessness with grime. I half expected a zombie to come down one of the halls, followed by a whole army of them, hell bent on making us one of their own.

"This is giving me the creeps, big-time," said Ben. He kept working his hands into fists, like the climb down had really set off his arthritis. "Are you sure it won't open if you push on it?"

"Dude, I'm sure," Alex said. He'd decided not to inject himself, shaking his legs awake instead. "She's not letting us out."

"I bet she will if we find the vials," I offered

halfheartedly. Right after I said it I thought the same thing they probably did: *how exactly is she going to know if we find them?*

"Let's fan out in teams of two and see where these tunnels lead," Connor said, leaning in pretty close to Kate as his chosen partner. "Three directions, six of us—meet back here in like five minutes. Maybe there's another way out or a way to contact her from down here."

"I'm not going anywhere," said Ben, "except back up there to pound on that door."

Alex stood up, rubbing his legs.

"I'm telling you, man, it's totally locked. And I already pounded on it a bunch of times."

"Well, I'm not going down one of those halls, no way," said Ben.

Marisa moved closer to him and put her arm around his shoulder. "I'll go with you. We'll protect each other."

"With what? Our shoes? Your smile? What if something's down here with us? I'm not doing it."

But Marisa pulled him toward her, which really bothered me. "Come on, we'll take the best-lit way. It'll be easy. We just have to find this room, get what we came for, and she'll let us out. No worries."

"Hell with that," said Alex, looking down the

passageway that remained, the one he'd have to go down with me as his partner. "I'm going with you guys. Light is my friend."

The three of them seemed to think if they got to the best-lit way first they'd have won the advantage to check it out, which turned out to be true.

"Fine, I'll take Connor and head this way," said Kate, pointing down the corridor with the red arrow on the floor and a sputtering light somewhere around a corner. Connor was game, and before anyone could start moving, the two of them were laughing nervously, holding hands like two people in a slasher movie about to walk into a very bad situation.

"Looks like you got the bad draw," said Alex, pushing Marisa and Ben down the second round passage, the one with the blue arrow and the pretty good lighting, and smirking at me like I was the big loser in this equation. Which I was. The one remaining hall, with the green arrow, was basically pitch-black. There were no lights down there at all, just curved walls of rusted metal that were quickly devoured by total darkness twenty feet in.

"You know what, I'll go with you guys," I said.

"No, we got this fair and square," said Marisa. "Just go, take a quick look. We'll meet back here."

Her eyes said it all. *You had me, Will. You really did. But I can't trust you, not for a while anyway.*

"Marisa, seriously—I'm sorry. I didn't know what else to do."

She didn't answer, unless you count those brown eyes looking back at me like I'd made the biggest mistake of my life.

"You guys would have done the same thing," I said, feeling the fear of being alone rise in my throat as they kept on.

"No, I wouldn't have," said Ben.

"Me neither, bro, me neither," Alex agreed.

Marisa turned back for the briefest of seconds, and I had a glimmer of hope that everything would be okay. Her resolve was starting to melt. I knew this girl. I could win her back if I played it cool for a few hours. And I could see how tired she was, which was to my advantage. She needed my protection the most when weariness set in.

I heard the distant echo of Connor yelling back from around a corner where I couldn't see him: "Nothing yet! You guys?"

"Nothing!" yelled Alex.

Only ten minutes had passed since we'd been locked underground and I'd been ditched by my girlfriend and everyone else. I stood alone for a few seconds, glancing down both rust-infested tunnels, thinking about taking chase down one of them. Then I pulled out the thing that Mrs. Goring had given me and took a closer look at it.

"What is this, a hotel?" I whispered to myself, barely hearing my own voice. It was a key card, green with a white arrow running down the middle. And there were words running down one side of the card, also in white:

GREEN ZONE OBSERVATION. SECURITY LEVEL: 4

"Just my luck," I said. "Green would be the darkest one."

The one nobody else would choose.

It was starting to feel like Mrs. Goring had set me up from the start, all the way back when she'd told me the truth about Rainsford and the cures a year before.

I thought about calling everyone back to me. It stood to reason that I held in my hand the key to a room that would hold the vials we were supposed to retrieve. But a bigger part of me felt like this was my chance to redeem myself. They'd find nothing, locked doors at the ends of tunnels, probably, and I'd find the treasure we sought. I'd find what we needed, get us out of here, and better yet, get them all cured. They'd be sorry they ever treated me like a disease.

I started down the hall with the green arrow on the floor and was stunned by how quickly it became disorienting and dark. My hands touched the ridges of metal and it made me think of a Slinky laid out along the carpet in my room. Looking back, I could still see a faint light shining around the hole that led up and out of the underground. Turning a corner would mean total darkness.

I'm going to find these vials and show these guys, I thought.

You tell 'em, bro! Keith's sarcastic voice filled my head.

You're darn right. I got this.

I started moving faster, hands in front of me like a blind man, and soon found another wall. This one felt like the surface of an empty swimming pool, smooth and flat, and it ended in a hard turn to the left.

I was dangerously close to feeling like I might get lost in the dark and end up starving to death or killed by the unseen creatures I felt sure were lurking everywhere.

In the distance I saw something small and green and glowing, like the soft light of an exit sign at the end of a darkened hall. It was lower than an exit sign, doorknob height, and when I reached it more quickly than I'd expected, I understood what it was.

I held the key card in my hand, turning it over like an ace of spades, staring at what looked like a Visa card reader stuck to the wall. In the soft glow of green from a strip of light on the reader, I could see the thick handle of a sturdy metal door.

"I'm so finding these vials," I said, elated at the prospect of getting the job done that no one else could take credit for. I was equal parts exhilarated and afraid as I slid the card through the reader like I'd done a thousand times before paying for groceries at Walmart with my parents. The locking mechanism on the door clicked solidly, as if whatever bolt had just moved was meant to keep everyone on the planet out.

I swung the door open and found that it was heavy, like the bomb shelter door in the basement of Mrs. Goring's place.[7] It was dark inside—too dark—so I stood in the doorway, hoping my eyes would adjust with the help of the paltry green glow from the card reader.

"Well done, Will Besting."

"Whoa!" I yelled, my shoulder flying sideways and connecting with the doorjamb. The pain was sharp and hot, but the shock was nothing compared to having heard Mrs. Goring's voice from inside the room. I

---

[7] I spent a lot of time in Mrs. Goring's bomb shelter. If you want to see what it looks like, I have pictures: www.willbesting.com. Password: *bombshelter*.

started backing away, stumbling over my own feet.

"Come inside," Mrs. Goring said. It sounded like she was in the room, walking toward me.

"Turn on the lights and maybe I will."

"I can't turn on the lights, Will. They turn on when you close the door."

"Where are you?"

"Does it matter? Just come in. You're very close now. Don't you want to save your friends? You owe them that much, after lying to them."

"I didn't lie to them! I just . . . I didn't tell them every little detail."

"And you spied on them, too. Didn't you, Will? You spied on your friends."

"I don't care!"

And I didn't, not about most of them. What did it matter anyway? But Marisa, that was different.

"I didn't want her to be afraid," I said, taking one step into the darkness. "I didn't see the point."

I'd dug into her files and listened to her deepest, darkest secrets. And as if that weren't bad enough, I'd deliberately chosen not to tell her what I knew about the cure. How do you not tell your girlfriend that stuff?

"I don't think that's the way they see it. I mean really,

Will, come on. You lied, withheld, cheated. You'd have to murder them for it to get any worse."

"You're a bad person, Mrs. Goring."

"I've been called worse."

I heard someone yelling my name from far away. Was it Marisa? I couldn't tell for sure, but I was done dealing with Mrs. Goring alone.

"Down here!" I yelled. "Down the green hall. I found the room!"

"You didn't find anything, Will Besting."

"Shut up, Goring!" I yelled. "Just leave me alone."

I heard someone coming toward me in the dark, maybe several people, yelling about who I was talking to.

"I will not leave you alone, Will. I can't. You're the way in. It's you and me now, to the end."

"What are you even talking about?" I pleaded.

"Get in this room right now."

"I won't!"

"You will. Or your friends will die."

"What? Wait—what are you saying?"

"Get in this room, Will Besting. Get in and shut the door. Their lives depend on it."

"Mrs. Goring, please. Don't do anything stupid."

"This is your last chance. If you want to get your friends

outside again, including Marisa, you better get inside and close the door *right now.* I won't ask you again."

My head was spinning with information, most of which I didn't understand and for sure didn't want access to. Why me? Why is it *always* me?

It was Marisa, I could hear her now as she came closer.

"Marisa, can you hear me?" I said, standing in the doorway.

"Yeah, I can hear you. I think we're almost there. Wait for me—don't move."

There was a sweetness in her voice, like she was afraid for me, like she'd missed me. But more than that, like she herself was trying desperately to reach me because she didn't want to be down here without me.

"Time's up, Will."

Mrs. Goring's voice had changed to a gruff whisper only I could hear. All I could think of were the words she'd said and the wild look in her eye when she got really angry.

Get in this room, Will Besting. Get in and shut the door. Their lives depend on it.

I stepped all the way inside and took the door by the edge, feeling its steel smoothness on my palm.

"I love you, Marisa. Don't forget, okay?"

There was some laughter—Ben or Alex or both—and then silence as I swung the door shut hard and fast.

The last thing I heard before the door closed all the way was Marisa's voice.

"I won't forget."

And then she was gone and I was alone with Mrs. Goring.

═══

The room filled with light when the door sealed shut and I had to shield my eyes for a second or two. I heard the iron bolt lock into place from somewhere deep inside the wall, followed by the sound of someone pounding on the door from the outside. It was a distant sound, and their voices were even farther out of my range of comprehension. The world had gone audibly soft and unfocused outside the room, and I turned to see what kind of prison I'd found.

"If you can't hear me as well as you'd like, use the big round dial. The one that looks like it belongs in a science-fiction movie."

Mrs. Goring's voice was back.

"Give them a little time, they'll start moving around. Like mice trapped in a maze."

She wasn't talking to me, or at least it didn't seem like she was, not just then.

"You can see them?"

"Sure I can. So can you."

The room had six monitors inside: four on the wall directly in front of me, plus one on each of the side walls. Below the monitors there were control panels from what did look like a 1950s science-fiction movie. And there was the dial, below the center monitor on the far wall, just like she'd said. The monitor above the dial crackled to life and there was the bottom of the ladder, where we'd come in.

"This is starting to feel familiar," I said, walking to the dial and turning up the volume on Mrs. Goring.

"Too loud," she boomed into the room, and then with an audible click the screen changed and there she was, staring at me. The entryway on the screen was gone, replaced by wicked old Eve Goring. She controlled the monitors from the outside, or at least some of them.

I cranked down the volume to a reasonable level, then spoke:

"If you hurt Marisa—if you hurt *any* of them—"

"You're hardly in a position to threaten me. Better you listen and do as you're told."

I screamed in frustration and pounded my fists on the metal door, then kicked it way too hard and screamed again from the pain. I sat on the concrete floor and felt like sobbing with anger. Sobbing from being controlled, for being dumb enough to fall into a trap, for fear I'd lost Marisa for good.

"Stand up, you coward," Mrs. Goring said. "You've got work to do."

I looked around the room once more and saw the dark, frosted glass above Mrs. Goring's face in the monitor, where a camera had to be positioned so she could watch me. I made a mental note to find something heavy so I could bash the glass in if the need arose.

You wanna play games? I'm good at games, I thought.

I don't know, bro. This ain't air hockey. She's a crafty old warhorse.

Thanks for the vote of confidence, Keith.

"Here's what you need to know," said Mrs. Goring. "It's dangerous down there."

"Ya think?" I mocked. From what little I'd seen of the surroundings, there were a thousand different ways someone could get hurt. "What is this place?"

"It was a missile silo, a long time ago."

"Liar."

"Oh no, I'm definitely not lying. You'd be surprised how many abandoned underground facilities like this there are. We were a jumpy bunch, back in the day."

"And I'm in the observation room?"

I had managed to find the place where my key card would be inserted; unfortunately, the mechanism for accepting the card had been destroyed.

"I hit it with a hammer. You can't get out, Will. Not unless I let you out. And that's not happening until you get what I sent you down there for."

"The vials."

"Yes, the vials. And like I said, it's dangerous. There will be obstacles."

"Like what? Rats?"

"Worse," she said, turning my sarcasm into something I was actually worried about. I watched the monitor as Mrs. Goring disappeared and the screen returned to a view of the entryway. They'd returned there, and I tried to pick out Marisa in the group, but the camera was far away, so they were just bodies milling back and forth.

"There are still some, shall we say, *hot* locations down there."

"What do you mean, hot?"

"Nuclear. It's why they put these things underground,

Will. Also why I don't swim in the pond."

"Are we being nuked down here, Mrs. Goring?" I couldn't think of any other way to ask a serious question.

"Only if you enter the wrong rooms or open the wrong doors. Watch the dials—they'll tell you if someone has gone someplace they shouldn't."

I walked up to the control panel and found a series of round dials like speedometers on a car dash with words under them.

GREEN ZONE LEVELS

RED ZONE LEVELS

BLUE ZONE LEVELS

O ZONE LEVELS

The needles were all hovering softly around the number 2 out of a total of 10. At 6 the numbers turned red.

"There are also some electrical problems," Mrs. Goring said. "Look to the left of the door, there's a schematic."

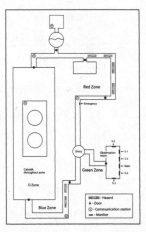

I turned and saw a tattered piece of paper about a yard wide with zones and rooms and passageways. There were hazard lines all over it.

"The lines indicate places where the floor has caved. There's a lot of electricity pumping through the water in those holes. Keep your friends clear."

When I turned back in the direction of the monitors, Mrs. Goring's face had returned. She'd moved from being only heard to being seen again, which had an unexpectedly calming effect on my nerves. Seeing her made me feel closer to the surface, closer to getting out alive.

"Look familiar?" she asked.

Part of me wanted to put my fist through the glass surface of the screen. She was staring at me like she held all the cards and knew it. And she was referring to the room she was in, which did look familiar. She was standing in the bomb shelter. Obviously she had more control over those monitors than I'd had a year before. My guess? There was a hidden panel of buttons I hadn't been aware of, controls she would now use to communicate with me at the times of her choosing.

"So you don't see a problem with one or more of the six people you sent down here falling in a hole and getting fried?"

"Not really, no."

"Is there a chance someone might find a drum of atomic sludge?"

"Only if they open the wrong doors, and you control the doors."

That was interesting. Apparently I controlled the locks on the doors, which meant I could also limit where everyone could go.

"Any bombs down here?" I asked, moving in closer to the monitor, trying my best to remain calm while I searched the space around her head for anything that might help me get out of an abandoned missile silo.

"They've all been dismantled, but some of the parts are still down there. Someone much smarter than you might even be able to piece something together if they had the right tools."

Yeah, I thought. *And shove it down your throat.*

"And you think I'm just going to agree to help you find these vials?"

"It's your call, Will."

"And it's your war with this guy, not ours."

"I'll find someone else to do it if you won't. But your friends won't last long without your help. There are a lot of wrong turns down there. I know the right turns; the ones that will keep them alive."

I yelled at her and fell heavily against the door with my back, sliding down to the floor, where I sat staring at the concrete.

"Calm down, Will. They're not going anywhere until you unlock the doors."

"Why are you making us do this?" I pleaded.

"I already told you. So I can kill Rainsford."

"But you don't even know where he went! This is insane."

"I have little doubt that he'll be back. It's only a matter of time."

I stood up, reached into my pocket, and felt the thing that I had found in the woods.

He's already back, you fool.

He's back and he's going to kill you first.

I didn't know for sure he'd returned, but it was a possibility. One thing was for sure: Mrs. Eve Goring wasn't alone at Fort Eden.

She looked at her watch and then back at me, an icy resolve in her voice.

"You don't have a lot of time. Hours, not days, Will."

"What's that supposed to mean?"

"There's no water down there you'd want anyone to drink. And there is some radiation, trace amounts, but enough to cause some problems if you stay too long."

"I'm not telling them that."

"I figured as much. You do like your secrets, Will."

Maybe she was right. Maybe I did like holding my cards close to my chest, but what good would it do them to know they were gulping down mouthfuls of deadly air with every breath? It would be panic. Better they didn't know.

"How long do I have to finish this errand for you?" I asked.

Mrs. Goring glanced at her watch again, and when I expected an answer, she turned to the left as if surprised by something. I thought I heard a knock, but I couldn't be sure where it came from. Was it from outside the observation room door or from the bomb shelter?

"I have to go," she said nervously. "Open the blue door first and send two of them through. *Only* two, no more. Once they're on the other side, lock them out. Don't send anyone else yet. The controls are self-explanatory. Do as you're told and this will all be over before you know it. I'll check back in half an hour."

"Wait—I'm not locking anyone—"

The screen went dead before I could finish what I was going to say, and I listened as the muffled pounding outside the door continued.

Mrs. Goring was gone.

3:30 PM—4:00 PM

I didn't really have a choice, at least that's what I told myself. She'd leave us all to die if I didn't get what she wanted. But I also didn't think it was going to be useful to freak everyone out by getting into the actual gravity of the situation. If I managed to get everyone out alive, I could tell them later, when less was at stake, and they'd forgive me. At least I hoped they would.

The control panel for the room was like a giant surveillance system switchboard. If it hadn't been for the hazardous situation I was in, I think I could have spent all day checking that thing out. It was retro-cool, covered in mechanical doodads that hadn't been touched in ages. There were clunky, round knobs begging to be pushed, and levers that looked like gearshifts for tiny race cars sticking out all over the place. Dials, meters, buttons, and red glass covering bulbs designed to light up and warn someone if the world was coming to an end. The door features were marked with helpful notations:

OPEN BLUE ZONE DOOR

BLUE LOCKDOWN

O ZONE LOCKDOWN

OPEN RED ZONE DOOR

RED LOCKDOWN

It was obvious that some of the controls opened doors while others automatically shut and locked them without anyone having to do anything on the outside. The reason for this kind of mechanism, I figured, was to act as a failsafe if an accident occurred and something nuclear needed to be contained, lest the whole place end up crawling with atomic energy. There were switches for the six monitors on the walls. Each had a number, and lining them up with the printed map against the wall by the door, I figured out what they were. These were communication devices, ways for not just me to talk to them but them to me. I switched them all on and found myself looking at empty corridors, wide open rooms, the entryway.

"Hey, you guys, over here!" I yelled, trying to lure them to a communication station where they could hear me. But they just stood in the entryway, looking confused and scared. I started clicking random switches on the console, yelling into the monitors.

"This way! Follow my voice! Hey! Hey!"

I could see them all standing around the exit, looking perplexed and saying things I couldn't hear, and then Connor seemed to understand as he pointed toward the red zone and ran off camera. Everyone followed but Ben Dugan. He watched them leave, then looked up the tube leading to the top of the way out.

"Don't do it, Ben," I said, but he couldn't hear me from where he stood. There was no audio, only visual at the entrance. "Don't be an idiot."

Ben started climbing up the ladder and out of my line of sight just as one of the monitors filled with four angry faces staring back at me.

"What the hell is going on, Will?" Kate asked.

"This is good!" I said. "I can see you. I can hear you. Can you hear me?"

"Where are you?" asked Marisa. She was curious and scared, her eyes focused on mine.

"You can see me, that's excellent," I said. "I'll be able to tell you where to go."

In hindsight, it was not the right thing to say at that particular moment.

"You're out of your mind if you think we're taking orders from you," said Alex. "Just answer the question—where are you?"

I searched the different monitors for signs of activity and saw none. Ben was still missing.

"I'm locked in a room at the end of the green tunnel. I can't get out and you can't get in—it's how she planned this. I had nothing to do with it."

"Oh really?" asked Kate, pushing Alex aside and filling the entire screen with her face. "It feels more and more like you two set this whole thing up. How'd you know to go down there?"

"I didn't—I mean, she gave me a green key card, but still—you guys left me . . ."

"Yeah, right. Whatever you say, Will."

"Either way, we're all stuck down here until we get the

vials and bring them to Mrs. Goring. That's the truth. I know as much as you do."

"Where are the vials?" Connor asked, leaning in close next to Kate, which made Kate move off as she rolled her eyes.

"Everyone just listen carefully, don't freak out—and first things first: if you see a hole in the floor anywhere do not—I repeat, *do not* get anywhere near those things."

"You're scaring me, Will," Marisa said. Everyone else started shouting about what a jerk I was and why didn't I come out there so they could hold me down and take turns punching me.

"I'm locked in, okay? I can't get out or I would. And Goring's not letting any of us out until we get what she sent us down here for."

"Why does this feel familiar?" asked Kate. "Us in the middle of a huge mess and you off somewhere hiding in a corner."

I didn't have time to fight with Kate and figured my best play was to dive right into the instructions.

"I have a map in here, it tells me where to go and how to get there. She's giving me instructions as we go. I'll relay them to you and before we know it we'll be out."

"No way I'm trusting you or that lady," said Alex. "No way."

He glanced around, searching for something, and mumbled to the others, "Where's Ben?"

"He's trying to climb out," I said. "I saw him go up, but he hasn't come down yet. I have a feeling he's not going to be very much use."

"Ya think?" asked Kate sarcastically. "He's barely holding it together."

"Just listen to me!" I yelled. The only way they could hear me was if the S1 button on the console was switched to the ON position when I was talking. I knew this because the next thing I said was "Shut the hell up, Kate!" after I turned that button to OFF.

"I can read lips, you know," she said, and this, for some reason, made Connor laugh.

I turned the audio back on.

"While we're on the subject of the area around the exit, I can't hear you guys from that position—I can only hear you when you stand next to one of these stations."

"How many stations are there?" asked Marisa.

"According to the map, there are five. Is there a metal box behind you, to the left?"

I'd seen the box on the map marked *emergency* and wondered what was inside.

"Yeah, yeah," said Connor, vanishing from the screen. A few seconds later I could hear but not see him telling me what was inside. "Two flashlights, and they work! And a first aid kit, too bulky to carry around."

"Great, maybe take some basics out—Band-Aids or whatever—the flashlights are an awesome find."

Things were looking up.

"Two of you need to go back to the entrance and follow the way toward the blue zone/O zone. That's what Goring told me—just two people, the rest will probably be going in the red direction, I'm not sure. And before you ask, I don't know why. On the blue side you'll find a door, which I can open from in here. Once I've got two of you on the other side, I can guide you to another communication station."

"What's on the other side of the door?" asked Connor. "What's the map show?"

"Hold on," I said, because, really, I had very little idea myself. I'd only had a few seconds to look at the map and hadn't really taken it all in. I backpedaled across the room while they took turns yelling instructions at me I didn't listen to. The blue zone/O zone led through the door and down another round corridor.

"I think maybe Alex and Connor would be best for this," I said, hoping mostly to keep Marisa safe from two hazard areas that ran along the path behind the blue door. There were two pitted-out floors in that direction, two chances to fall in and die.

"Must be bad," Kate said fearlessly. "Or you'd send your girlfriend that way."

"I'm not his girlfriend," said Marisa.

"Oh, I think you are," Kate said, grabbing Marisa by the arm and dragging her off screen.

"Marisa!" I yelled, but Kate had either overpowered her or talked her into it, because Marisa didn't return as Connor leaned his entire fat head into the screen.

"You want me to chase after 'em or what?"

A huge moment of indecision swept over me. Connor was the biggest and strongest of the group, so I wanted him with Marisa in case anything happened. But he was also vying for her attention, and being Connor, he presented a serious threat to my getting her back. And adding him would make three, which exceeded what Mrs. Goring had told me to do. It would be risky defying her orders.

I watched as Kate passed in front of the camera at the entrance and Marisa willingly followed, the two of them quickly past my ability to see in a few short seconds. The blue door would stop them soon enough, so technically I had as long as I wanted to think.

"Start by getting Ben Dugan out of that shaft before he falls and breaks his neck," I told Connor. "Let me look at the map again."

"Roger that," said Connor. He could be surprisingly agreeable when there was something important to do that required his attention. He and Alex took off down the hall and I used the few seconds I had to look more carefully at the red zone tunnel, which told me all I needed to know. That direction held even more hazards to fall into. I returned to the controls, trying to understand as fast as I could how everything worked. It wasn't like the bomb shelter, where only one monitor could be on at a time, and with all of them on it was mostly disorienting, too much information coming at me all at once. I realized what it must feel like to be a night security guard watching a bunch of black-and-white monitors of what essentially amounted to nothing moving. The images were all grainy, oversaturated color.[8] All six monitors projected views of haunted, unmoving space. Long, round passageways of rusted-out metal and missing sections of

---

[8] I did some research on this, and it turns out color TVs started arriving in the U.S. in 1953, but the programming lagged behind. Most people didn't have color sets until the late '50s, so networks just kept putting black-and-white shows on. The missile silo was built in the early '50s, or so Mrs. Goring said. The color monitors down there must have been some of the first of their kind.

floor, empty rooms strewn with garbage and manuals and old office furniture, a wall of closed doors, giant empty spaces with looming, curved silos. It was the view of a place forgotten, filled with a hundred ways to die, crumbling slowly and silently into oblivion.

I forced myself to look away from the monitors and focus my attention on the map one more time. I took a deep breath, really drinking in the whole of the underground facility.

Marisa and Kate would be standing at the blue door, waiting for me to open it. Connor and Alex and Ben, they'd be leaving the main entrance and going back to the communicator near the red zone door.

While I was lost in the details of the map, a familiar voice filled the observation room without warning.

"Send the two girls together, they'll be fine."

I felt a blinding urge

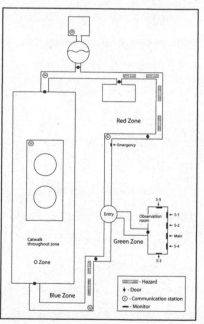

to rip the door open, but of course I couldn't, and turning around I saw that Mrs. Goring had returned.

"I'd appreciate it if you could stop sneaking up on me like that. It's freaking me out."

"You've been down there for almost forty-five minutes. Progress needs to speed up."

"I'm working on it," I said, watching her but also watching the other monitors in case Connor and Alex returned. "Which way is safer, blue or red?"

"Smart boy. You see by the map there are two ways around."

"Just answer the question, will you?" I asked, peering back at the map and running a finger along the red path.

"Red is safest," she said.

I'd come to see Mrs. Goring as a liar and a cheat. I didn't trust her.

"Why do I have to close the blue door once they're on the other side?"

She wouldn't answer me and seemed, once again, distracted by something I couldn't see.

"Only one door can be open at a time," she finally said, her attention returning. "That's the trick. Otherwise you get a wind tunnel full of something you don't want to be breathing in. It's especially true once you open the O zone."

As best I could tell, the O zone was comprised of a gigantic room at the end of the blue tunnel.

Still, blue was safest, not red. I felt it in my bones.

"Once you get two of them on the other side of the blue door, get the rest through the red door. Same thing, close it when they're through. I'll be back with more instructions. Don't fail me, Will. I'm watching."

She was gone in a flash, and the central monitor switched back to a view of the entrance, which seemed to be its resting position when Mrs. Goring wasn't bothering me with instructions. There I saw Connor and Alex, yelling up into the tube, trying to coax Ben back down to earth.

"There has to be a way to turn on some audio in there," I complained.

I flipped switches and turned dials but there was nothing, just silence from the place where we'd entered, but I did discover something important in all my tinkering. The switches for the cameras swiveled, which I hadn't realized at first. Each switch had a round knob sitting on the end of a metal rod—the shape and size of half a straw with a marble for a head—and swiveling one to the side like a joystick, the camera whirled slowly into a different position. It was like moving the side mirrors on my mom's car back home.

From looking at the map I knew there was a communication station on the other side of the blue door, so if I opened it and Marisa came through with Kate, I could move the direction of the S2 camera and I'd see them both. It was all I could do not to press the large, round button that would send them through, because I knew what I'd have to do once they stepped away from the door.

I'd have to engage the BLUE LOCKDOWN option and throw the door shut again, sealing them off on the other side.

My hand hovered over the blue button, big and round, like something the president would push in order to launch a missile attack.

You have to get her through, Will, I thought. *She's safest on the other side. Just put her through!*

My hand hit the button hard and I felt it click under the weight of my palm.

Had it worked? Was the door open? I didn't know for sure until I saw them stepping cautiously through. I saw them on a monitor, slowly inching forward into a long, empty tunnel.

"Can you guys hear me?" I yelled, watching them in the S2 communication feed.

"Take it down a notch," Kate yelled back. "No need to scream at us."

"Sorry—move away from the door, but not too far. Don't get near the broken-out flooring."

"Why not?" asked Marisa. God, she sounded tired. I knew her well enough to know it was only a matter of time before she slumped down in one of the tubes and passed out for an hour.

"Because there's electricity in the water down there. It's not safe."

"Very nice, Will!" yelled Kate, but she and Marisa had moved away from the door, peering down into the muck of the first broken-out section. Kate had one of the two flashlights Connor had found and she pointed it down the tunnel in my direction.

"Don't move, just stay right there," I said. "And don't be mad, okay?"

"Too late," said Kate. But I was talking about what I did next and how angry I expected them to be. I pushed the button marked BLUE LOCKDOWN and heard the door slam shut behind them. Both girls screamed, then they returned to the door and tried to pry it open as Kate cursed me in a long, flowering echo.

I couldn't look from the shame of what I'd done, and I found myself staring at the entryway, where Connor and Alex were looking up into the exit, still trying to coax Ben Dugan down. They were waving and yelling, until something shifted in their perspective that made them stop what they were doing and jump out of camera range. About two seconds later I saw what it was: a falling body, which landed in a heap on the tile floor.

Ben Dugan, with his arthritic hands, had lost his grip. And by the looks of the situation, it had happened quite a way up the ladder. Both Connor and Alex were quickly at Ben's side assessing the damage, but I only got a brief look at them before the screen fluttered crazily and the feed went dead. I looked at Kate and Marisa and saw that Marisa had slumped down on the concrete near the door, her head hanging as if she'd fallen asleep.

"Looks like we're taking a little breather," Kate said, and she sat down, too.

The video feed on the main screen started popping back to life, accompanied by the sandpaper sound of static, but nothing could have prepared me for what appeared on the monitor.

It was the bomb shelter, where Mrs. Goring had been.

That part hadn't changed, but Mrs. Goring wasn't sitting there anymore.

The world underground was in chaos, but up above, in the gloom of Fort Eden, someone else was staring back at me.

4:00 PM–5:00 PM

4:00 PM–5:00 PM

"Who are you?"

That was the first question she asked me, and I asked her the same thing right back. We had a silent standoff for all of five seconds, her staring at me and me back at her. Even in the fuzzy glow of a fifty-year-old monitor, this girl was cute. Blond hair pulled back with a royal blue bandanna that matched the color of her eyes; brilliant white skin, like porcelain, and a delicate nose.

"I'm Amy. Are you one of us?" She was looking around

a lot, like she was nervous someone might find her.

"Umm . . . I don't think so. I'm Will. Why are you at Fort Eden?"

"You wouldn't understand," she said, and it seemed like she was about to leave, but then she took a deep breath, letting it out as she stared at the floor. When her face came back up, it was different. There was fear in her eyes.

"I don't trust her, something's not right."

I tried to ask what she meant but she just kept going.

"Where are you? Where am *I*?" she looked around the bomb shelter as if she had fallen down a rabbit hole into an alternate reality.

Amy was confused, and I had a feeling I knew what she was doing at Fort Eden. I wanted to talk to her, but there was no time—any second now Connor and Alex would show up on a monitor or Kate would start yelling at me. Or worse, Mrs. Goring would come back to the bomb shelter and catch Amy standing there.

"Did Dr. Stevens tell you to come here?" I cautiously asked.

"Yes! You *are* one of us!" She wasn't yelling, she was whispering excitedly, so I read her lips more than actually heard her words. Amy moved closer to the monitor, still warily turning back to the door of the bomb shelter again and again. "She's your doctor too, right? Are you getting cured?"

". . . Not exactly," I said, trying to buy some time. "I mean, maybe. I don't know."

"It's scary, right? I'm not sure I'm doing it. She's not what I expected."

"Who?"

"Mrs. Goring. She's, I don't know. I mean she's the best, right? Some sort of miracle worker. I just don't know."

"How did you get into her basement?"

"Easy, I walked."

Her answers left a lot to be desired.

"How many of you are there?"

"You have a lot of questions, Will."

"Sorry, it's just . . . listen to me. Don't let her know you found this place. She won't like that you're talking to me."

"Why? Are you bad?" She laughed nervously, but then she asked me again: "Where *are* you?"

Before I could answer she was off the screen, as if someone had called her away; then she was back, but only for a second.

"I have to go, but I'll come back. Don't go anywhere. And Will?"

"Yeah?"

"There are seven of us."

She reached up and touched the royal blue bandanna holding her hair back, then her hand hovered near the screen as she shut it off, and the place where Ben had fallen was back. The camera held a steady, unmoving eye on the place where we'd entered the underground missile silo. It was the same as before, only it wasn't.

Ben was gone. So were Connor and Alex.

I glanced at Marisa and Kate on S2, where they were still resting, then threw every monitor switch into the off position as fast as I could. I needed a second to think, to piece things together in my head without being distracted. I couldn't control the central monitor—that was on but silent, pointing at the exit. But other than that, it was a moment of complete isolation from the rest of the world.

I reached into my pocket and fished out the thing I had found in the woods and stared at it. It was soft, torn at the edges, not very big: a royal blue strip of bandanna, same as the one holding back Amy's hair.

They can't be serious, I thought.

The only explanation I could fathom was that Mrs.

Goring had figured out how to use the fear chambers and the equipment in order to do for herself what Rainsford had done so many times before. She'd instructed Dr. Stevens to bring seven more subjects to Fort Eden. Amy was one of the seven, she would be the first to be cured. And over the next seven days, Eve Goring would use Amy and the other six to get what she wanted.

She would use them to become young again.

═════

There were gaps in my understanding as I stood in the surveillance room staring at the floor. Big questions lurked in the dark corners of my mind as I prepared to turn the monitors back on again.

How long before Amy and the other six would start getting cured? If it was like it had been for us, Mrs. Goring would start the cures as early as that night, six or seven hours later. That didn't leave me much time to sort things out.

Had Mrs. Goring really figured out how to use Rainsford's twisted tools of immortality, or was she simply going to experiment on these people and hope for the best? It was a tragic situation either way, because they'd all end up in the fear chambers regardless. Could I let that happen?

And why, really, were we being held captive in an abandoned underground missile silo? I was beginning to doubt Mrs. Goring had any intention or ability to actually help us. All she wanted was the vials. Did she need them in order to complete some part of her own process? Or did she really intend to cure us and kill Rainsford if he ever came back?

All these thoughts and many more washed over me as I was jolted back to reality by the muffled sound of someone pounding on the door outside. The door had the echo of something ten feet thick, the deadened hum of Connor's voice barely piercing the space between us.

He was mad, that much I could tell.

I switched on all the monitors and saw that Kate was standing again, pulling Marisa up with her.

"Just leave me here," I heard Marisa mumble in a half-stupor.

"No such luck, sleepyhead. Wake up!" Kate shook Marisa and yelled over her shoulder. "You back, Will?"

"Yeah, I'm back. Hang on a sec."

"We're moving with or without you, so you better

hope she doesn't fall asleep on her feet and end up in one of these holes."

"Hey, I'm not *that* bad." Marisa was waking up, coming out of her cocoon.

The S1 monitor, where I'd first called everyone, was filled with Alex's face. He said something about what an ass I was and ran off screen in search of Connor. With Alex's head out of the way I saw Ben Dugan sitting against the metal tunnel, his head slumped to one side. They'd dragged him down the passage while I wasn't watching.

"Ben, buddy, how you doin'?" I asked.

"What's wrong with Ben?" Marisa asked from S2, and I was happy to hear some spunk had returned to her voice. The ten-minute nap had revived her.

"Idiot smashed both of his ankles and messed up his back." Connor had returned, and hearing the question, he'd answered it for me.

"How bad is it? Can he walk?" I prodded.

"No way. We'll have to carry him out of here."

"If we get out at all," said Alex. "It's starting to feel like there's no reason for us to even be down here. Did she tell you anything else?"

"Wait, so Ben is okay, just incapacitated?" I pressed.

"I'm fine, Will. Just get us out, okay?" Ben had lifted his head with some effort, staring up at me. "It's mostly my feet that hurt, like I sprained both ankles at one time playing soccer or something. I can just sit here."

Alex's face tipped into the monitor from the side: "Let's finish this thing so we can vacate before someone else gets hurt."

"Answer Connor's question," Kate insisted. "Did she give you any more instructions?"

"There are two wide holes between you and me, or you and the monitor anyway. There's a corner at the S2 monitor, and beyond that, another door I can unlock. I need to get you guys behind that door."

"So you can lock us even deeper down here?" Kate mumbled, but she didn't push it and I didn't answer. Instead, I turned to Connor and Alex, who stood next to each other staring at me.

"You guys need to get through the red door, down the hall. Once you go through I'll close it automatically, so step aside. And don't give me any grief about locking it behind you—it's what I'm being told to do. I'm only following instructions, which is our best chance of getting out of here. Keep going once you clear the door, avoid holes full of water or anything that looks like it might electrocute you, and eventually you'll come to another doorway to your left and a hall to your right. Skip those and keep going. I'll see you coming."

I'd seen the doors I described on the map and didn't really understand where they led to. One entered an unmarked space about the same size as the room I was in, the other to something more mysterious, a large circle and a square behind that. It didn't matter, because Mrs. Goring's meaning had been very clear: *Don't open doors I don't tell you to open. Some are better left closed.*

"We're past the first hole, Will, no worries," said Kate, sounding closer in the echo chamber of the tunnel at S2. "But the next one's bigger."

They were standing on the edge of a space of tiles that had crumbled apart and fallen into darkness below. Swiveling the camera I could see pipes and frayed wires poking up through the rust-colored water.

"Give me a second to think, don't go yet."

I slammed the knob that opened the red door and got the salute sign from Connor as he moved off camera and Alex took chase.

"Tell me when you're through!" I yelled.

"Hell yeah!" Connor answered. The more I worked

with this guy, the more I envisioned him as a sergeant on the ground, guiding a battalion into all sorts of trouble on sheer adrenaline. He was the kind of guy I'd likely be in favor of having as my captain in a situation like that. Too bad he has senile dementia and won't get into the Marines no matter how hard he tries.

"Hey, Will."

It was Ben, from the floor, his eyes a vacant stare.

"Yeah, I'm here."

"Do you think we're getting out of this situation alive?"

He said it loudly enough for Marisa and Kate to hear it from where they stood, the audio feeds bouncing in and out of the room to other parts of the facility. It was a lesson learned: not everyone needs to hear everything.

"Wait, what's wrong with Ben?" asked Marisa, alarmed and confused. "Ben? Ben! What happened?"

"He's fine. Banged up a little bit, nothing to worry about."

"What do you mean, *banged up*?" asked Marisa. "Will, this is crazy. What are we doing down here? Tell her to let us out!"

"I demand that she let us out every time I see her stupid face!" I yelled, frustrated by the position I'd been put in. "And just as soon as she shows up again, I'll ask her another time. But I can tell you based on what I've been dealing with—it's not going to change her mind if she knows one of us is hurt."

"So banged up is hurt. What happened?"

"Marisa, he's fine—right now I need you to focus on getting down that hall as slowly and carefully as you can."

"Stop treating me like you're in charge or something. I'm just worried about Ben."

"Ben!" I yelled, and he nodded his head toward me, staring up into the camera like there was a flashlight in his face. "How you doin'? You okay?"

"Yeah, I'm good. Just tired. Back hurts. But I'm fine."

I turned to Marisa in her monitor and made a face that asked whether or not this was sufficient enough evidence for her.

"This isn't easy for any of us," Marisa said, and then she turned away, putting her hand against the curved wall, staring off toward Kate. Without my consent, Kate had started working her way along the edge of the watery, electric hole of death.

"Take it easy, Kate," I said.

"We're on the other side, Will!" shouted Connor.

"We've cleared the door!"

"Standing clear!" said Alex, attempting to fit in or mocking Connor, I couldn't tell which.

They sounded like they were on a mission with a stated objective of setting off major explosives and blowing things up.

I engaged the red zone emergency lock and heard the door slam shut, losing contact with Connor and Alex until they wound their way through the labyrinth of tunnels and found the next station.

"Kate!" Marisa screamed.

When I looked back at S2, Kate was wobbling along the edge of the tunnel, having lost her balance. Marisa had gone along the other side of the long hole in the floor, and leaning out, caught hold of Kate before she was forced to step forward into an electric charge she'd never recover from.

"Marisa! Don't move!"

The two girls were holding each other's shoulders, leaned in, facing one another as they stared down into a wide mouth of death.

"Just take it slow. Reeeal slow," I said.

"You didn't answer my question," Ben said from S1. "Do you think we're getting out of here alive?"

"I'm a little busy right now, Ben. Gonna have to get back to you on that."

I shut Ben's monitor off and focused every ounce of my attention on Kate and Marisa. I zoomed the camera in at their feet, panning back and forth over the water.

"I think you should keep going, just like that. Pushing off of each other might not work."

"Don't go falling asleep on me," Kate said to Marisa, and she took one tentative step sideways, then another. Marisa mirrored her movements, but on the third step the tile broke free and fell heavy, like a flat boulder, into the hole. Sparks of electricity flared up and water splashed on Marisa's foot. Both girls went into a brief spasm as an electrical charge jumped through the water and died, but not before giving them both a jolt.

"Don't let go!" I yelled as the side Marisa was on gave way and vanished in front of her. More sparks flew, more water splashed on both girls, more jolts held them together like electrified glue.

The center monitor crackled alive and Mrs. Goring appeared, calm and elusive as ever. The timing of her arrival was maddening, but her demeanor ticked me off even more: totally calm, as if nothing terribly important was going on.

"Looks like you're not doing too well. Maybe I picked the wrong guy for the job."

I ignored her.

"You guys back? You okay?" I asked. They were both breathing heavy as Kate looked up at Marisa.

"Your fingernails are digging into my skin. Mind backing off on the grip of steel?"

"Sorry—it was—sorry," Marisa said.

"She'll have to jump to the other side. It's the only way," said Mrs. Goring, again with a voice like she was doing her nails on the other end, bored out of her skull.

I hated to admit it after looking at the situation, but she was right. The floor on Marisa's side of the tunnel had collapsed entirely, and there was no place else to go.

"The walls are curved out, she's got room. Just tell her to jump."

"We can hear you, Mrs. Goring," said Kate. "Can you hear us?"

"I can."

"When I get out of here I'm going to beat the hell out of you."

"Better bring a baseball bat. I'll have my ax."

"Shut up, you two! Just shut up!" Marisa screamed.

She was crying as she screamed, not hysterical, but close.

"It's only three feet across. Jump. It's easy." Mrs. Goring was nauseatingly calm about the possibility of my girlfriend getting electrocuted to death. But it sort of helped settle Marisa down. I could see her and Kate whispering quietly, probably about how they were going to kill me and Mrs. Goring when they could get their hands on us and how Kate wouldn't bring a baseball bat to do it—she'd bring a chain saw.

All at once Marisa was airborne, jumping over the hole and landing hard with her face against the curved metal side next to Kate.

"Will, listen to me," said Mrs. Goring. "Shut off their monitor."

"No way I'm doing that!"

"Shut it off or I'll never let them out. Do it right now."

"Marisa, you're close! A few more steps is all. I'll be *right* back."

"What do you mea—?"

Her eyes were pleading, looking at me like she couldn't believe I was about to leave her out there on her own. It was one of the hardest things I ever did, cutting that feed.

"I hope you know what you're doing," I said. "If she dies down here—"

"What, Will? What will you do? You'll stay down there, too. It doesn't do me much good if someone gets killed down there either, you know. You all get out alive or I've got a murder on my hands. More mess to clean up. It's a lot of work. Do you understand what I'm saying, Will?"

I did, and I couldn't believe the thought had only just occurred to me.

"If one of us dies, we all die."

"Bingo. Can't have the rest of you up here giving me grief about a dead body in the basement."

"You're sick, you know that?"

"I'm not the one in need of a cure."

I was trading insults with a seventy-year-old woman and it was getting me nowhere.

"We're all going to live, I can promise you that," I said. "Tell me what to do next."

Mrs. Goring appeared to be looking at a different monitor, her attention split as she mumbled to herself, then turned her gaze back on me.

"Go to the map, I'll tell you a few things."

"Not until I see if they made it."

"Fine, make it fast and then turn the damn thing off again. I need your undivided attention."

I switched on the monitor just long enough to see that both Marisa and Kate had made it across, then shut it off again before they could start yelling at me. After that I took a quick look at the S4 communication station in the red zone and saw nothing but a long, round corridor with intermittent light. Connor and Alex had two holes to maneuver before turning the corner, and there was an added problem of water dripping everywhere. It would be slick, slow, and dangerous. I might not see them for a while or ever again.

"What am I looking for?" I asked, turning my attention to the map.

"Send Marisa and Kate into that big room, the one with the silos. It's also called the O zone."

So that's what those circles are, I thought. *Places where they used to keep bombs.*

Then she said, "The floor in there isn't safe."

"I'm not following. You mean more holes or what?"

"They're not going to want to go in there when they see it, and I don't think you're going to be able to convince them. You don't have it in you."

Mrs. Goring was basically driving me insane. Cool, collected, and completely off her rocker. I tried to veer the conversation back to the floor.

"Mrs. Goring, what's wrong with the floor in that room?"

It was more of a hangar than a room, ten times as big

as any of the others, a vast football field of empty space.

"Time's running short," she said, glancing at some relic of a watch on her pale, thin wrist. "I'll have to tell them what to expect, but first, before you bring them back online, about Connor and Alex."

"Yeah, about them," I said, moving my line of vision to the section of the map where they'd be arriving soon. "They should be showing up in that long corridor with the rooms any time now."

"There are two rooms on that hallway. It's very, very important that you get this right, Will. Your life depends on it, and so do theirs. The room on their left can be unlocked from the outside. It was designed that way, to keep things in, not out. Don't let them go in there. You don't want what's trapped behind that door escaping into the hall.

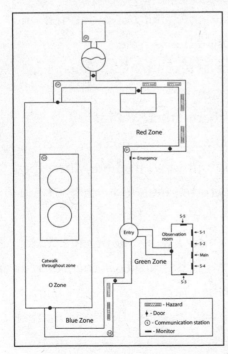

Red Zone

← Emergency

Entry

Observation room

S-5

S-1

S-2

Main

S-4

Green Zone

S-3

Catwalk throughout zone

O Zone

Blue Zone

▭ - Hazard
♦ - Door
◎ - Communication station
━ - Monitor

The door is vacuum-sealed, tight as a drum. As long as you don't bother it, you and your friends will be fine."

"Great, more nuclear waste, just what we needed."

"The door on their right will lead to an important place. It's marked *Silo 3*. Do you see it on the console?"

I returned to the console, leaving the map behind, and saw a flashlight beam at the end of the long tube where Connor and Alex were scheduled to appear.

"They're getting closer," I said, and crossing the room to the console, I found what Mrs. Goring had mentioned. "And I see the door lock release for Silo 3 marked with an X."

"Good boy. You might work out after all."

God, I hated Mrs. Goring.

"Now, put the girls back on. I have something I need to tell them that will interest you as well."

Against my better judgment, mostly to see Marisa and make sure she wasn't too mad at me, I opened the signal again. I could hear Connor and Alex yelling from down the hall, an echo of *We're coming! Hang tight!* Etc. etc. The good news was that Kate and Marisa were actually laughing. Seeing and hearing two multiple feeds at once was a little like standing in the hallway of an insane asylum: laughter and shouted words carried in from reverberating corridors, and the horrible Mrs. Goring overseeing it all.

"Turn Connor and Alex off," said Mrs. Goring. "Their lack of common sense is distracting me."

I complied, at least in part because I couldn't concentrate with Connor and Alex yelling about their slow progress every two seconds either.

"I'm glad to hear you're having such a good time, girls," said Mrs. Goring, and this put a quick end to Kate and Marisa's celebrating over cheating death or whatever it was they were laughing about. "I need you both to keep going, through the next door, into the O zone. It's just a few steps farther down the hall. There's a second camera there, in the big metal box on the wall. It's attached to a cord that will run about a hundred feet. Take the camera with you or I won't be able to tell you what to do once you're on the catwalk. Will, when they turn it on, it will replace the feed. If they turn it off or it dies for some reason, the feed will reconnect with the S2 station. Understand?"

I nodded, yeah, but Marisa said what we were all really wondering about.

"Catwalk?" Marisa asked. "You mean like up in the air?"

"Clever girl. You can't walk on the floor in the next room. You'll see why when you get there." Mrs. Goring thought twice about what she'd said and added a little more: "You two don't always hear me loud and clear, so here it is one more time: do *not* walk on the floor in that room."

"Let me ask you something, Mrs. Goring," Kate said. She put her face right up in the monitor so her striking features warped in weird directions. "On your mother's grave, which I imagine is located somewhere out behind the Bunker where you bury all the bodies, do you swear these vials will actually help me get rid of these headaches? Because you know what? They really, really hurt. And this little errand you've got us on isn't helping any."

"And yet you laugh," said Mrs. Goring. "Such a strange girl."

"Laughing keeps me sane, but it won't keep me from killing you if this is all for nothing."

"I do love your spunk, Kate Hollander. And here's your answer: I'm telling you the truth. Bring me the vials and I'll end your pain. I can do it, but I need what he took from you."

Kate paused meaningfully, as if she was trying to discern the hint of a lie in Mrs. Goring's answer, and then she looked steely-eyed into the camera. "Lead on, Mrs. Goring. Me and sleeping beauty here are itching to open that door."

"Yeah," said Marisa, and though it was a tired *yeah*, it was deep and sincere.

"On the other side of the door, you'll find a vast, open room. Breathe softly when you enter and climb the ladder attached to the wall at the door. The ladder empties onto the catwalk. It's not in very good condition, so choose your steps wisely. And watch the cord from the camera; don't let it touch the floor."

"If there are rats on the floor I'm not doing it," said Marisa.

"There are no rats. They wouldn't last five minutes in there."

"That's encouraging," Kate said, staring in the direction they were expected to go.

"There's a smaller room on the ground floor, under the catwalk. It's the only one. Two silos extend out of the room and through the ceiling. Get as close to the silos as you can with the camera, then wait."

Kate reached her hands above the screen and jostled my view back and forth a few times, freeing the mobile camera from whatever held it firm against the wall. I watched as Marisa coiled the long black cord around her arm like a sleeping serpent.

"Oh, and ladies?" Mrs. Goring said. She couldn't see them because their monitor was on the same flat wall as Mrs. Goring's, but she could hear them preparing to leave. "If you turn back or try to trick me, I won't let you out. Not ever. And I'll cut off communication between you and Will."

Marisa didn't say a word, but the resolve on her face grew tenfold. I, on the other hand, was in the mood to throw up. What would it be like to die alone, completely isolated from anyone else? It's moments like those that make me realize who really matters. I'd be okay right up to the end if I could get there with Marisa. She'd make it okay, but I'd have to die first. I was lost in this idea of dying alone or dying with the one person I loved the most when Marisa spoke.

"We're going to do exactly what you ask," said Marisa. "And then you're going to let us out of here and we're never coming back." She looked straight into the camera and gave Mrs. Goring the finger. And by finger, I mean *the* finger. Mrs. Goring turned off her connection, and the laughter vanished abruptly as the screen turned empty and still.

"Marisa—" I started to call.

"Don't, Will. Just don't."

"You heard the girl," Kate said, leaning her face down into my view. "Leave her alone. In case you hadn't noticed, we're about to enter a room where the floor might eat our legs off. She doesn't need your drama right now."

Things were bad enough without me getting into deeper trouble with Marisa, and even though I was mad at how unfair I thought they were treating me, I focused my attention on other things and left them to their task alone.

Mrs. Goring was gone, but in my head I could still hear the tone and the quality of that horrible voice. It was not a pleasant recollection bouncing around in my head as I fired up S4, expecting to see Connor and Alex making their way toward me.

"They should be really close by now," I pondered. "Where the heck are they?"

Seconds passed in which I looked at the map, the door, Ben Dugan, the tunnel where Connor and Alex should have been.

"Will? Hey, boy in the locked room, out here." It was Kate, waving at me, close and wobbly.

"Where's Marisa?" I asked, because I couldn't see her.

"Just shut up and listen. Is the old bag gone?"

"Yeah, she's gone," I said. I thought of telling Kate about Amy, but there was so much going on so fast I couldn't imagine getting into it with her. Who I really wanted to tell was Marisa, but she was never alone.

"I'm done trusting her. And so is Marisa. She has no intention of letting us out."

"I'm working on that," I said, thinking of Amy and how she might be able to help us if I played my cards right.

"She likes you best," Kate said. "Try and trick her into letting you go and then hit her over the head with a rock or something. Use your charm on her."

"Is that like a joke?"

"It's the best I could come up with on short notice."

Marisa came back into the screen, and I smiled unexpectedly. She glanced away, then back at me.

"You doing okay?" she asked without a trace of a smile.

"I'm fine, and I'm going to get us out of this. I promise."

Another pause, a deep breath.

"You better. How's the hearing holding up?"

"Huh?"

"Funny boy. No really, okay?"

"Yeah, not bad. I can crank the volume in here pretty good."

It felt good to talk to her, but she was guarded. I couldn't tell if she was trying to forgive me or if Kate had put her up to being nice so I'd get my head on straight.

I looked at the monitor where Connor and Alex would soon appear, but they were still a no-show.

"Hang on a sec," I said.

I pressed the audio feed into the lock position for S4, so Connor and Alex could hear me yelling.

"Where are you guys? Hey! Connor?"

"We're going," Kate said impatiently. "We'll take you with us as far as we can. And Will—get us the hell out of here, okay?"

"I'll try my best. Remember what she said—don't drag the cord on the floor."

"I think she's trying to scare us is all," said Marisa.

"Yo, Will!"

It was Connor Bloom, calling from somewhere down the tunnel, but I couldn't see him. What the heck was going on?

"Hang on you guys, I'll be right back."

I killed what was now the mobile S2 feed that Kate was carrying around with her and stood directly in front of the S4 monitor, searching for Connor and Alex.

"Where are you guys?" I yelled. "I can't see you."

"Hang on, bro! We're checking something out."

Checking something out? What did he mean, checking something out? There weren't very many things to check out, just the long tunnel, holes of death in the floor, sputtering lights, and . . .

"Connor! Alex! Show yourselves! Where are you?!"

I ran back to the map, searching for anything I'd missed, some cavernous tunnel that branched off the main line or a hidden room. But there was nothing.

Connor and Alex were either down the short hall that led to the circle and the square behind it on the map. Or they'd done something really, really stupid.

Hadn't I told them not to open any doors on the way? I thought I had, but there was so much happening. Maybe I'd forgotten to do it. I looked at the radiation level dials and saw that they hadn't moved.

Two figures stepped out from the shadows just as I was about to reconnect with Kate and Marisa and tell them that I'd probably managed to unleash a major nuclear catastrophe in the underground missile silo.

"You guys scared me half to death! Please tell me you didn't open that door."

Neither Connor nor Alex answered me as they kept coming closer. It was really dark in that last stretch leading to the monitor, but that didn't mean they couldn't hear me. I tried again.

"If you opened that door go back and shut it! Answer me!"

"You can stop yelling, Will. It's not going to be a problem with the door. You worry too much."

They were close now, within ten feet, and the tunnel made the voice sound eerie and unfamiliar. Something wasn't right. The next thing I remember was how close his face was, how he looked happy to see me, how he thanked me for letting him out of the room.

It was Davis who stood there, the man who was once Rainsford, not Connor. And not Alex, either. It was Avery who stood next to Davis. Avery Varone.

Connor and Alex had opened that door and let out something dangerous, all right. Had I told them not to open that door? Did I somehow confuse them so they thought they were *supposed* to open it? Really, it didn't matter.

Rainsford and Avery Varone were in the underground missile silo with us.

And we'd just let them out into the open.

5:00 PM—6:00 PM

5:00 PM — 5:30 PM

Two hours.

120 minutes.

7,200 heart-pounding seconds.

That's how long it took me to accidentally let the vil-est person on the planet out of a room that, obviously, Mrs. Goring had somehow managed to lock him inside of. It would have helped if she'd been straight up with me about what was in that room. Then again, she'd been pretty clear in her own twisted way:

Your life depends on it. . . . You don't want what's trapped behind that door escaping into the hall.

How she'd gotten Davis-who-was-Rainsford and Avery in there was kind of beside the point. They probably came back to check on things, she held Avery at gunpoint, she forced Rainsford to open the door for her, she made them climb down the ladder into the room, she locked the door—something along those lines made pretty good sense. I know I wouldn't mess with Mrs. Goring if she were pointing a shotgun at Marisa. Chances are Rainsford would have been the same as me in that regard.

What really mattered, what ate away at my soul while I stared at his perfectly chiseled face, was that I'd let him out. I'd let him out where he could get to Marisa, where he could get to everyone.

I'd been able to hold it together for two hours as things unfolded in unexpected ways all around me, and standing there I took command of the situation in the only way I knew how: I turned Rainsford's monitor off before he could infect me with his lies.

For a brief moment the observation room was silent and I took stock of the situation.

Ben had fallen and lay half comatose on the floor of a tunnel. I had to get him aboveground soon or risk having him go into shock. I remember thinking I could actually lose this guy if I screwed things up. He was saying he was fine, but all evidence was to the contrary. He was in some trouble and getting worse.

Marisa and Kate had narrowly avoided electrocution. They had a mobile camera in a room with a floor that could not be walked on. As bad as that sounded, they were maybe in the best shape of anyone in the underground missile silo.

Connor and Alex, my crack commando team, had lasted all of twenty minutes on the move and ended up locked inside a room where they were completely useless. I couldn't help thinking Davis—who was really Rainsford—had done a lot of bad things. And he was desperate, looking for a way out just like us. Could he have already killed Connor and Alex? The guy had been alive a long time. He probably knew ten different ways to kill two teenagers with his bare hands. It was possible.

Mrs. Goring could return to the observation room main monitor at any moment. I had to be cagey, clever, on my best game. Above all, I couldn't let her know that Connor and Alex had accidentally let Rainsford and Avery out of that room. She'd be furious. And I couldn't let her know I'd discovered her diabolical plan. Seven new subjects, only this time, she'd try to work the same trick on herself.

I was in contact with a girl named Amy. She was oblivious to what was really going on, but she was on the inside. She might show her face again, she might not. Amy was a wild card, maybe my best chance at getting everyone out alive.

As I stood there breathing, staring at the switch that would bring Rainsford back, I thought about Amy. I wondered what her fear was. And what about the other six? What were they going to be cured of? And then I had another, far worse string of thoughts.

Mrs. Goring isn't going to let us out of here. She's trying to get rid of us, to erase all evidence. There are no vials.

I hit my palm against my forehead four or five times, trying to shake the bad thoughts out of my head.

You don't know what Mrs. Goring is up to. Be careful, Will. Don't do anything foolish. Don't fill in blanks where you're not sure of the answers.

Being locked inside the central nervous system by a madwoman did have one advantage: I knew everything while no one else did. But it was a big responsibility. I had to be careful with what I knew and who I told. Rainsford didn't know about my special knowledge. He would assume I was like all the others—a blank slate when it came to the cures. He would play it as if he was Davis, a guy who'd been through the program himself. But I knew the truth: Davis and Rainsford were the same guy. And this guy could not be trusted. No matter what happened, I had to remember some basic facts: Rainsford was a liar and a cheat. He was clever. He'd tricked a lot of people before. He might kill me if I let him get too close.

I had to think about every word I said, connect all the dots, find a thread that would lead up and out of the missile silo.

And so it was that when Rainsford spoke to me for the first time in the missile silo, I was not forthcoming with information. I turned the monitor back on, watched as he gazed up at me with piercing eyes, and prepared to be evasive.

"Hey, he's back!" Rainsford said, calling Avery to his side. "We thought we'd lost you."

"No, I'm here. Just a glitch with the wiring—it happens."

The faulty wiring would be an excuse to go offline whenever I needed to.

Nice thinking, bro. You're smarter than you look.

Thanks, Keith. You don't know how good that makes me feel.

Don't mention it.

"Where'd you come from?" I asked.

"I don't even know where to start," Rainsford confided, and I felt the stream of lies coming before he even said them. "We came back, you know, to see how Mrs. Goring was doing. She freaked out, something about vials down here we had to retrieve for her."

"And she locked you in?" I asked.

"Looks like she tricked you, too," Rainsford said. "I think she's unstable."

"What was your first clue?" I joked.

His voice didn't have the Rainsford hypnotic quality I remembered. Maybe his powers of persuasion were locked inside a much older version of himself.

"Hi, Avery," I said, looking past Rainsford to the shadowy figure behind him. "You doin' okay?"

She wouldn't speak, just a nod and half a smile. Avery Varone didn't look well. She was pale as a ghost, except for the circles under her eyes. Those were dark. Everything else about her face looked like the blood had been sucked clean out of her, leaving only a fragile shell for holding a confused girl. And it wasn't just her face, it was her hair, too. That was the most shocking part about the new Avery Varone. The streak of white had spread. All of her hair was white. The dark eyes, the pale skin, the white hair—she was a ghost, or something like one.

"How long have you been down there?" I asked. Avery looked up doe-eyed at Davis like she needed approval to give the answer, and he reached out, holding her frail hand.

"Long enough," he said. "I'm doing okay, but Avery, she's not taking to the surroundings. We need to get her out of here."

"What's wrong with her?" I asked. Avery leaned forward into the camera before Davis could stop her.

"I'm fine, Will. You worry too much." Her papery voice and vacant eyes made me nervous. She was even weaker than she looked.

"What did Goring tell you?" asked Davis. "Did she say she would let you out?"

"If we get what she sent us down here for, she will."

"I can help with that," he said. "I know where the vials are. Rainsford told me. Tell me where you are and I'll come to you. We can figure it out from there."

Yeah, right. Like I'm going to trust you. Nice try, I thought.

It was bizarre knowing Davis was Rainsford, hearing

him talk about himself in the third person.

"Can I ask you something?" I said.

"Sure, anything."

Davis kept glancing at Avery, then back at me, like he was trying to make sure she didn't give me a signal of some kind while his back was turned.

"Where are Connor and Alex?"

There wasn't any getting around the fact that two people were missing, and I began to wonder why Rainsford wouldn't have just brought them with him to the monitor. Something wasn't right.

"Insurance," said Davis, his face changing ever so slightly in the monitor. The old Rainsford was in there, screaming to get out. He didn't like having to hide.

"I don't follow."

"I know you have special awareness, Will Besting. I can see it in your eyes. You know who I really am. Avery does, too. Don't you, sweetheart?"

My cover was blown, but the cool thing was I didn't care. There would be no pretending, no dance about what he knew and what I knew. He'd dropped all pretense of being Davis, so I'd be dealing with the real Rainsford, straight up, no games. I doubted he'd planned to drop his cover so fast.

"Okay, *Rainsford*. I'm going to ask you once more," I said, trying to gain the upper hand. "Where are Connor and Alex?"

"I didn't expect such bravado, but you always were unpredictable."

"Just answer the question."

"They're in the room where I left them."

"So they're alive?"

"Did I say that?" he looked at Avery, a dark smile on his face.

"Avery, you know this guy is like a thousand years old, right?" I looked past Rainsford's hypnotic stare, trying to rouse Avery's attention. "He's not Davis. There is no Davis."

"It's not what you think, Will. He helped you, he helped all of us. He watches over me."

"Yeah, looks like things are going really well for you. Did you help him kill Connor and Alex?"

"They're not *dead*. He's not like that."

Avery looked at young Rainsford like he was all she cared about in the entire world. She'd fallen under his spell. But she'd tipped their hand, too. Connor and Alex were locked in a room, a room I might be able to get to if I played my cards right. I looked at the locked door behind me and the smashed card reader hanging from the wall.

Leaning forward into the monitor, I put my hand on the switch that would kill Rainsford's feed.

"Don't go anywhere."

Rainsford tried to answer, but the signal went dead before he could say a word. I was in control, not him, and I planned to keep it that way. I switched on Kate and Marisa's feed and dialed up the volume.

"How you guys doin'? Everything okay? Can you hear me?"

I could see they still had camera cord to spare and that they'd made it into the vast chamber and up onto the catwalk above. There was a weird hue of hot color rising off the bottom of the lens as Marisa's face appeared close and fast.

"Stop leaving like that!" she yelled. "We've been sitting here waiting for you for like an hour."

I looked at my watch—it had been nine minutes—but it didn't feel like the right time to argue about where I was or how long I'd been gone.

"Sorry, it's just . . . well, it's complicated is all. There's a lot to keep track of."

"Show him," Marisa said, looking over the lens where

Kate held the camera. She was obviously upset, but I didn't know why until the camera tilted downward and I saw why the bottom of the lens had been glowing with radiant light.

"Welcome to the fun house," said Kate. "Got any advice?"

"What the hell is that?" I asked.

Kate was quick with an answer that wasn't very useful: "From up here, it looks radioactive. You want me to throw my shoe down there and see what happens?"

"Not funny," I complained. Sometimes I wished Kate would either shut up or get serious. The constant smart-ass treatment got old.

"We think it's some sort of sponge because it has that, you know, squishy look to it. Like it's been soaking up nuclear gunk for fifty years and it's just sitting there, waiting to be disturbed."

It did look like there was a layer of dust on the surface of the entire floor, but something was underneath that showed through in some places. The whole thing had a bizarre orange hue that glowed with toxic energy. It was like the moon, with mounds of dust piled up in some places, lunar-like craters of spongy flatlands in others. Now I knew why it was called the O zone. O was for orange.

"This is a bad deal," I said, furious all over again at Mrs. Goring for sending us down there. "Why on earth would she even need to be in here?"

"What else did she say, Will? Can you call her or something?"

Marisa had taken to lying down on the catwalk, speaking straight up into the air.

"She said something about getting into the silos, remember? But not how we'd be able to do it. Can you see the room?"

"We're right over the top of it," said Kate. "We got that far on the catwalk. But we can't get inside. Oh, and your girlfriend just fell asleep, so there's that."

"Let her rest for a few minutes, I'll be right back."

"Will, no! Don't—"

It was a pleasure cutting Kate off in mid-sentence, something I could imagine enjoying all day long if I had time to kill. I was sorely tempted to do it just one more time—it would have lifted my spirits. But then I thought about Marisa and how she needed those little catnaps. Having Kate yell at me might wake her up.

I stared at the map for a few seconds, trying to see a way into the silo room, but it was a fairly basic construct that neglected to show anything other than the one doorway in. Mrs. Goring had to know of another way, why else would she send them in there to begin with?

I had thought Kate and Marisa were in the safest place, farthest away from a monster who had been set loose underground. It turned out they were perched over a radioactive ocean, twenty feet above the most dangerous place in the whole missile silo.

5:30 PM–6:00 PM

I crossed to the door and pulled out my Recorder, which included a small compartment along the side where I kept two tiny tools, important when you're a guy that's constantly tinkering with electronics. Both tools were long and skinny, made of titanium, with hard rubber grips in the very middle. On one end of the first tool there was a minuscule Phillips screwdriver, on the other end a star-shaped pattern with a flat end. The other tool was the same, but the ends were a flat-blade screwdriver and a sharp, razor-thin knife. I couldn't help thinking about the ways in which I could put these tools to use as weapons against Rainsford and Mrs. Goring if given the chance.

You're not much for blood sports, bro. Put the knife down.

Not now, Keith. I'm busy.

You know it's true. Mowing down soldiers on my Xbox was a stretch for you back in the day.

It was true. I wasn't a killer, not even in a video game. For all my talk I knew it would take everything I had to stick a knife in someone, even if that someone really deserved it.

"Let's see what we're dealing with," I muttered, switching my attention to something I could actually do as I slid my Recorder back into my pocket and approached the busted door-lock scanner. It hung on the wall by one wire, the others having been cut, and the mechanism itself had been hit with a heavy object enough times to render it useless. The casing was pretty well smashed and the insides were tumbling out of one side like cooked spaghetti. There was also an exposed circuit board, which had been broken into two halves, and a fuse with the glass broken out.

"Interesting," I said.

Without a working fuse, no amount of power would find its way through the wires even if I could reattach them correctly, but overall, the situation was not insurmountable. I got the Recorder out again and used the star bit to remove a section off the back, revealing a series of tiny colored wires attached to a circuit board on my homemade device.

"What are you doing?"

I whirled around, scared half to death by the sound of a voice, and expected to see Mrs. Goring watching me. She'd figure out what I was up to and threaten to leave me down here forever if I didn't stop. But as I turned, stuffing things in my pockets as fast as I could, I saw that it wasn't Mrs. Goring after all. It was Amy, the girl from before. The girl with the blue bandanna.

"Nothing, I'm—I'm just bored I guess," I lied, still not knowing if I could completely trust her. "Just wishing I could get the door open, looking at this broken card reader. But it's a total loss."

"It's Will, right?" she asked. "That's your name?"

"Yeah, Will Besting."

She got very quiet, so I walked closer and asked her a question.

"Amy, when do the cures start? Did she tell you that much?"

"Yeah, she told us. They start tonight, I don't know what time though."

I looked at my watch, already after five PM. I had a few hours to get aboveground.

"I said I'd go first," she said, laughing softly. "Crazy, right?"

"I wouldn't do that if I were you. Let someone else have a go, then you can see what they say. There's always tomorrow."

"Yeah, we're here for a week, so I guess there's no rush?"

"Totally. No rush at all."

"Actually, Will?" she said.

"Yeah?"

"I'm kind of thinking of not doing it. She scares me."

"Look, Amy, just hold tight, okay? And come see me as often as you can as long as you're sure she won't catch you. And keep an eye on things up there, watch what she's doing."

"Did it hurt?"

Our eyes locked. She wasn't ready to get off the subject of the procedure, and I knew what she meant: had it been painful when I was cured. It was a hard question to answer, but I'd thought about it a lot over the previous year and I had strong enough opinions about it.

"My fear was about something painful I couldn't face. I buried it, but it was there. For me the procedure itself wasn't painful, but it made me face painful things I didn't want to. So I guess the answer is yes—it hurts—but not like you think it will, and not necessarily *when* you think it will."

She nodded a few times, slowly, like she was chewing on my answer. I didn't want to rush her, but I also couldn't stay offline with everyone else much longer.

"We might be able to help each other," I said, which brought her eyes back up to mine.

"How? I don't even know where you are."

"Have you been to the pond yet?"

"Only once, when we got here yesterday. She stuffed us in that stupid Bunker for an hour when you and your friends showed up, and now she makes us stay in the Fort and just sit around. She's in the Bunker right now, upstairs, making lunch or something."

"How'd you find the bomb shelter?"

"She goes back and forth all the time through the tunnel, it was actually pretty easy to find. I'm kind of a loner and there's a lot of dead time. People don't seem to mind when I go missing."

Amy and I had a lot in common, it seemed.

"Listen, Amy, I have to tell you something. Mrs. Goring calls me from that same room like once every hour. She might catch you if you're not careful."

"Thanks for the warning. I'll stay alert. She's not exactly quiet when she moves around in those boots, pushing that cart around. And she's always preoccupied anyway. I swear she could walk right past me and not even notice I was there."

Yeah, I thought, Mrs. Goring has a lot on her mind. Preparing for seven cures while keeping a bunch of people locked underground.

"Maybe sneak down to the pond once more, see if there's a padlock on the door to the pump house. Could you do that?"

Amy shrugged like she didn't have a clue.

"If I can get out, I'll do it. And Will?"

"Yeah?"

"Thanks for talking to me. I feel better."

"No problem."

"I better go."

"Yeah, okay—check back if you can on that pond thing, right?"

She nodded and the signal died.

I wanted to go back to work on the door lock, but I'd

kept a lot of people waiting too long already. Before I turned anyone back on, I thought about Mrs. Goring and the cures again. I looked at my watch and worried about how little time I had before Amy might be in her own fear chamber, undergoing the procedure. I didn't have much time and there was a lot to do. One more glance at the door—it would have to wait—and I fired up S1 so I could check on Ben Dugan. His chin lay heavy on his chest and he'd slumped into the corner like a rag doll. At first I thought he might be dead, a line of reasoning that put my brain into a tailspin.

No one can die down here, I thought. *That can't happen.*

I'm thinking it already did and now you've got a body to get rid of. Better hope a pack of rats don't show up.

Not now, Keith.

Hey, your problem, not mine. Just trying to help.

I yelled Ben's name three times before he jerked awake and stared up into the camera all bleary-eyed.

"You scared me half to death," I said. "Don't do that!"

"Sorry, just tired. And bored."

"Well, don't sleep too much. I think that might be bad, like you might not wake up or something."

"Whatever you say, Will. You're the boss."

"Making progress. I'll have you out of here before you

know it. How's the back and the ankles?"

Ben didn't answer and it seemed like he was drifting off to sleep again. I started yelling at him to wake up as Mrs. Goring appeared on the main screen with an impatient look on her face. I switched Ben's monitor off and let my hand hover over the control for S4, thinking about putting Rainsford back into play.

"You need to let us out," I said coldly. "I don't think Ben can walk and he's in a lot of pain. Plus he won't stay awake."

"Sounds a little bit like your ex-girlfriend. Maybe the two of *them* should date."

Something about her voice, the way it turned on the word *them*, pushed me over the edge. I slammed my fist down on the lever for S4 and brought the hallway to life. I was surprised to discover that Rainsford and Avery were gone. The hall was empty.

"Have the girls made it to the silo room yet?" asked Mrs. Goring.

"Uhh . . . yeah. Yeah, they're stuck."

Rainsford was coming up the hall toward me again, but this time he was walking fast, with purpose. He could hear Mrs. Goring's voice. He was holding one finger to his lips. *Shhhhhhhh.*

"Focus, Will. Focus!" yelled Mrs. Goring.

"Get us out of here, Mrs. Goring. I mean it. We need out."

Damn Rainsford! He'd come right up to the monitor, shaking his head slowly back and forth.

I'm not out here. Don't tell.

I felt like a pawn stuck between two competing monsters.

"You're distracted," said Mrs. Goring, "and demanding. I'm not happy about it. Put Kate on."

Mrs. Goring couldn't see Rainsford because the S4 monitor was on the same wall, she could only hear what was happening. I stared at them both, in possession of knowledge Mrs. Goring didn't have. He was right there, boring into the room with those powerful eyes of his, and Mrs. Goring didn't know it. As far as she knew, Rainsford wasn't holding a piece of paper up to the camera, close so I could read the words he'd written:

OPEN R1 NOW

He was asking me to open the door I'd used to let Connor and Alex in there in the first place. Opening that would give Rainsford access to the main exit, but he'd still be locked underground like the rest of us. There was something about Rainsford that close to the outside that made me nervous. Who knew what tricks he had up his sleeve?

"Turn S4 off, Will," Mrs. Goring said. "It's distracting you. I need you to concentrate on Kate and Marisa."

She was asking me to kill the signal at S4, and just as I was about to do so, Rainsford slid the piece of paper up on the lens so I could see the entire message he'd written.

OPEN R1 NOW

OR CONNOR DIES

I wasn't about to have someone else's blood on my hands. I hit the camera switch for S4 and the door-open knob for R1 at the same time, which turned Rainsford's feed off and opened the R1 door simultaneously.

I'd done what both of them had asked of me. Whatever happened next, at least I'd complied with their demands.

"Focus, right here," Mrs. Goring said, pointing a jagged finger at her temple. "Just keep Connor and Alex where they are for the moment. They won't be waiting long. Unless Kate and Marisa have fallen off the catwalk, they should be ready for instructions."

"They're fine, they're waiting."

I fired up the mobile camera, which had been set down. It gave off a view of the orange glowing floor through metal grating, but Kate and Marisa were a blur off in the distance.

"Kate?" Mrs. Goring yelled. "Tell me exactly where you are."

"Don't drop me!" Marisa screamed, and I suddenly realized what was going on. While I was gone they'd ventured farther out on the catwalk than the cord would take them. From what I could tell, Kate was lying down on the metal grate, reaching down into the open air.

"Grab my other hand!" Kate shouted.

"I told them not to go past the length of the cord," said Mrs. Goring. "I did tell them that. You heard me."

"Shut up!" I screamed. "Kate? Where's Marisa?"

She wouldn't answer, but I could see something moving below Kate, legs dangling in open air above a sea of radioactive gunk. It would swallow Marisa whole if Kate dropped her. Her skin would melt off, she'd go into a seizure, and the floor of this disgusting room would eat her alive.

Keith's voice boiled up in my head.

Bro, that is some sick thinking.

But it could happen. What should I do? Keith, you're the gamer. What should I do!

No instructions for this one. No cheats. Your girlfriend is about to go zombie big-time.

I watched in horror as whatever section of grating

Kate was lying on top of lurched downward about two feet, sending Kate sliding forward with it. She wrapped her legs around one of the metal pipes holding the catwalk to the ceiling and jerked to a stop. I waited for the plume of orange dust that would rise into the camera lens as Marisa fell and hit the lunar landscape of death.

"Stop moving!" Kate screamed. "I'm not letting you go!"

"Hold on, Kate!" I shouted, then I turned to Mrs. Goring on the main monitor. "Can you get me out of this room? Let me save them!"

"You've got the only key card," she said matter-of-factly. "Send Ben in there, see what he can do."

"Ben can't walk! I told you that. He's useless."

Mrs. Goring looked to her right and then back at me.

"If you can get this mess under control, there's a sliding door on the side of the first silo. Inside that there's a ladder down into the room. Have them look on the side of the mobile camera—there's a key duct-taped to the bottom—that key will get them into the silo room once they climb down."

I was barely listening as she said these things. My attention was mostly on the fact that Kate and Marisa were not moving. They appeared to be holding firm in one position, quietly talking to each other. The catwalk ran the entire length of the giant room, with the exception of the huge round silos shooting up through the middle. If the map was correct, then there was another room on the ground floor, below the catwalk. It would be smaller, big enough to hold the base of both silos. A quick glance at the map gave me the lay of the land once more.

"I have to go, but I'll be back. Look at me, Will. *Will.*"

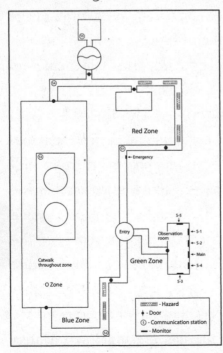

I shook my head as Mrs. Goring got my attention back and I stared into her stone-like face. She wasn't moving, just staring, and when she did speak, it was void of emotion.

"If Marisa doesn't make it, we'll have to regroup. I need two people in that room one way or another."

And just like that, she was gone. The idea of losing one of us hadn't registered at all, except as a possible alteration to her plan.

"How long can you hold on, Kate?" I yelled.

There was a long pause, then a breathless response.

"Hang on!"

I waited for about five seconds, watching as Kate slowly worked her way back around like a gymnast on the slanted section of grating.

"No, no, no. Can't be . . ."

Kate was up on her feet, walking rapidly toward the camera. Soon, all I could see were her feet.

"I know what you're thinking," she said. "But she's not dead. Not yet anyway."

"'Then where is she?"

"She's hanging on, Will. And I heard everything Goring said."

She leaned her head down into the camera as she picked it up.

"Now I gotta go. I'll see you when I see you."

And with those words, Kate vanished. She'd either ripped the camera cord out or simply turned it off. Either way, I had no idea what her plan was or whether I'd see her alive ever again. Kate was either going to save Marisa or she wasn't, and I wasn't being invited to watch the proceedings.

I screamed into the room, angry and frustrated beyond anything I'd ever felt. I went to the door and pounded on it, kicked it, yelled at it. If I could just have gotten out I could have gone to her, gone to them both, maybe done some good. But I was trapped without a prayer in the world of getting out on my own. Marisa's feed had gone dead, and no matter how many times I pushed the lever to bring her back, she wouldn't return.

I switched on the S4 station and gazed at the dripping walls of the tunnel. It was empty for a moment, cold and silent. Rainsford's face drew into the screen from the side, fast and close, and he yelled sharp and quick. Then he laughed, because I had screamed, too, taken by surprise. I wanted to kill this guy but knew I couldn't. Mrs. Goring had tried many times over many years. He'd lived ten lives, maybe more, and no one had ever been able to bring Rainsford to an end. It was maddening to think about. I would grow old, I would suffer death. In the end, he would always have the last laugh, which was what his laugh sounded like, a reminder of the facts.

It doesn't matter if I'm locked down here. I'll get out.

Watch me. And when I do, I'll make sure you grow old and die and I don't. I win. I always win. Everyone else loses. They all lose in the end. Including you. Ha Ha Ha.

What was I going to say? There was nothing *to* say, that was the problem. He was right. So I turned off the monitor, which was the only sane thing I could think of. Talking to him would do me no good.

I engaged the S1 station so I could at least see that Ben was still alive and feel like I wasn't totally messing every single thing up. It struck me then that I'd opened the R1 door, the door leading into the red zone where Rainsford who was Davis waited for me. I'd sort of let that slip my mind with everything else going on.

Looking into the tunnel at S1, I discovered more things to worry about as the world underground turned darker and more dangerous by turns.

Ben Dugan was gone.

And in his place?

A white-haired, hollow-faced girl staring up at me like a ghost.

Avery Varone, Rainsford's chosen one.

6:00 PM—7:00 PM

6:00 PM — 6:30 PM

I slammed my fist down against the control that closed the red zone door, sealing Rainsford on one side and Avery on the other. I'd been underground for 240 minutes; four hours in a room all alone watching the world come unglued. My mind was spinning with thoughts as I stared at Avery and her at me, neither of us speaking. Even as I encountered this altered version of the girl I'd once known, the forefront of my mind was still flooded with thoughts of Marisa. Her monitor was a black eye staring back at me, like a deep tomb she'd fallen into and could never get out of. But there were other thoughts, too, and those began to surface more prominently as I continued staring at Avery Varone. She'd stopped looking at me and began wandering toward the red zone door, but she wasn't going anywhere. She'd be back.

Rainsford had obviously taken Ben somewhere, most likely to the same room Rainsford had been trapped in himself. He was amassing quite a collection of people in there.

And then there was Amy. I hoped against all hope that she'd listened to me and gone to the pond. If she could confirm that the door wasn't locked, maybe I could convince her to open the hatch. Everyone but Marisa and Kate were trapped behind one door or another, including me. Incredibly unfortunate that I held the only key card for the observation room and I was on the wrong side of the door. Marisa and Kate, if they were alive, were the only ones besides Avery in a position to make it to the exit.

And the last thought, which was brought on by all the others: *I have to kill Rainsford. I have to find a way. Even if I have to die down here with him to make it happen.*

"Avery," I said. I could see she had made it to the red

zone door and tried to open it up, even pounded on it a few times, thinking Rainsford might come back and get her.

"You're not going anywhere, not unless I open that door. And I don't plan on doing it anytime soon."

"He'll come and get me," Avery said, her voice echoing phantomlike against the ribbed metal walls of the tunnel. "He always does."

As she started walking toward me, I looked at two monitors, ones that had, as of yet, been dark and motionless. I'd tried to make out what was in them, but the rooms hadn't had enough light. To my left, one monitor was marked S3. It was the one I hoped would turn on if Kate and Marisa made it into the silo room and cranked on the lights. It drew my eye relentlessly, the darkness like a cloud I wished would part and reveal Marisa on the other side. And to my right, on the opposite wall, the S5 monitor, the most mysterious of them all. It was the one behind the circle and the square room on the map, also a dark feed that offered nothing but shadows and stillness. I had a guess about that room. It was there, I was sure, that the vials of fear blood were hidden.

And Rainsford was a lot closer to that room than I was.

"She's a monster," said Avery. She'd made her way back to the monitor and stared vacantly at me.

"Avery, listen to me. What do you remember about the cure?"

She didn't answer, so I went in a different direction.

"Davis isn't who you think he is."

She looked up at me and smiled sadly.

"He's Rainsford. I know, he told me."

She really did know, really understood.

"So then you know he's, like, pushing eighty years old."

"No, that's not right. He's a lot older than that."

"He told you?"

"Sure he did. He loves me. We talk about everything."

I glanced at the S3 monitor again, wishing it would come on and I'd see Marisa's face, know she was okay.

"You don't know him," I said, maybe a little too harshly, but thinking of Marisa and the ailments we had and everything we'd been through, I was angry. "He's using you. When you get old he'll leave you behind, just like he did Mrs. Goring."

"He never loved her!" Avery shouted. She may have looked pale and emotionless, but Avery had plenty of energy when it came to defending Rainsford. "She was always mean to him. Did she tell you she tried to kill him? More than once."

"I have a feeling someday you'll want to do the same."

"She's just jealous because he chose me. She's bitter, Will. Mean and bitter and terrible."

"And old, which is what you're going to be someday."

"And he will be, too. He's not doing it again. That was the last time. He promised me."

If it weren't for how I felt about Marisa, I would have said Avery was insane. But love could make people believe things that weren't true. I knew how she felt.

"Here's a news flash for you, Avery—he's said that to people before, including Eve Goring. He's lying to you."

"Shut up, Will. And open that door."

"Sorry, not going to happen. Consider yourself trapped until you come to your senses."

She folded her arms across her chest and stared at me as if she were capable of keeping her mouth shut for a thousand years. She had a lot of resolve, I remembered that about her. And I had to remember that in some twisted way she was under Rainsford's spell. She wasn't seeing the world clearly, the way it really was.

"How did you end up down here?" I asked.

She didn't answer.

I was about to start guessing when the main monitor flashed on and off several times and then settled on a face. Someone was back.

"Don't go anywhere," I said to Avery, and then I turned her monitor off and cranked the volume on the main feed.

"Who was that you were talking to?"

Amy was back, looking a little tired and concerned.

"One of the many people Mrs. Goring has trapped down here."

"Down where?" Amy asked.

"*Under* Fort Eden."

It was time to really start spilling the truth if I ever hoped to get this girl to let us out.

"You're serious? Like, how many of you are down there?"

"Every single person who went through the procedure last year that you're about to go through. We're all down here, and someday I'm thinking maybe you will be, too."

"Me? Why would I end up down there?"

"Because you're tangled up in this thing now, and it seems like people who get caught in Mrs. Goring's web have a way of circling back and getting into even more trouble."

There was a quick but meaningful silence as Amy weighed what I'd said, and in the space of seconds, I could see she was afraid.

"Amy, listen to me," I said. "You don't have much time. If you and the other six people there with you are going to get cured, it will happen fast. Once the first one goes, the rest only take a few days. And there's something you need to know, Amy. I've been cured. Everyone down here has been cured. And it's not what you think. It's bad, is what I'm saying. You shouldn't go through with it."

Amy looked at the door, darting to the right and off camera.

"Hold on, Will," she said, but I couldn't see her. She was gone for maybe ten seconds, in which I practically crawled out of my skin wondering if she'd been caught by Mrs. Goring and the whole thing was blown. Without Amy, I had absolutely no chance of getting Marisa and the rest free of the underground missile silo. She was my only hope.

"I've gotta go." She was back, looking nervous and agitated. "She's around more now, talking to us about tonight. I can't come see you anymore."

"Wait—did you visit the pond?"

She hesitated, like she wasn't sure how to answer.

"I'm sorry, Will. I don't think I believe you anymore. About the cures, I mean. I'm first and I'm doing it. I just have to get better."

It struck me then that I hadn't ever asked her what her fear was. Also, that I was losing her and had to switch strategies fast.

"Look Amy, I don't know what you're afraid of, but I'm sure it's something that's really hard to deal with."

"You have no idea."

"Well, I kinda do actually. My fear was terrible, too. And you know what? It's gone. So maybe you're right. In fact, you are right. You should get cured. It's weird, but it does work."

"You mean it?"

"Totally, yeah. But I want to talk to you about it when you're done, okay? I think you'll have questions and I can answer them. I mean, I've been there, right?"

"Yeah, you have. I'd like that. Sort of like an after-cure date."

Whoa. This was bad. Or was it?

"A weird cure date," I repeated. "You know what? I think that sounds pretty good."

"We could do it by the pond," she said.

"It's perfect," I said. "Only, I'm kind of stuck *under* the pond."

"Not for long. I went down there. It's latched shut, but there's no lock."

"That's great! So you opened it?"

She reacted to my overexcitement by putting her finger to her lips.

"Not so loud, silly!" she whispered. "I didn't unlatch it, but I will. Mrs. Goring is bringing us dinner in about an hour, then we have an hour break. After that she wants me to go into this other room and see my shrink. Then I get cured."

"So during that one hour after dinner, you guys are left alone?"

"We're left alone all the time, Will. She's either at the Bunker or down under the fort somewhere we're not allowed to go. There's this long, winding staircase she uses. And it's only like five minutes to the pond."

"There should be a latch you turn, no lock on the door going down."

"It's perfect! I'll get cured, then come back to the pond after. Can you get rid of your friends?"

She was immediately embarrassed by what she'd said and started backpedaling.

"I didn't mean that—it would just be nice to maybe take a walk at first. Without them."

"I'm sure we can make that work. It'll be great."

Two things struck me about this conversation as she

signed off and left me standing alone in the surveillance room. One, Amy was obviously under at least a minor form of mind control. Mrs. Goring had figured out how to use whatever system it was that made people forget and, in the lead-up to a cure, a little goofy in the head. Did Amy really think I was going on a date with her? We'd been held hostage underground all day. It's not like it would be business as usual if we got out. And second, she was kind of into me, and pretty, and I hadn't expected anything like that to happen when I showed up at Fort Eden for the second time.

I took out my Recorder and started taking more screws off the back. I always thought better when my hands were taking things apart or putting something together. It took less than thirty seconds for me to remove a second section of the back cover and start digging around inside the Recorder. I found what I was looking for—a tiny glass fuse—and popped it out, nearly dropping it on the concrete floor as it sprang free of the circuit board.

I spent the next few minutes trying to jerry-rig the fuse into the busted card reader near the door. It was the wrong amperage and the wrong size—too small on both counts—and I knew I'd be lucky if I got one shot at sliding a card through. I reworked a few dangling wires, completely removed the casing, pried the fuse holding closer together, and tried to pop the broken circuit board back into one continuous piece. Then I reattached the main wires from the wall.

"That's about all I got," I said to myself, and it didn't give me much hope. I could scan the card once and there was maybe a 50 percent chance it would actually do anything at all, a sliver of a chance it would open the door, and a 100 percent certainty that it would blow the tiny fuse. One shot, and not a very good one.

I went to the map, searching the space once more, trying to figure out where I'd go if I could get out. Was there any sort of plan to the maze of tunnels that could work in our favor? I got lost in that idea in a matter of seconds, scanning the rooms and corridors for answers, trying not to think about the world outside the door for just a few more seconds.

And then I heard a voice.

Will. Over here.

My first thought was a bad one. It was happening all over again. When my little brother died it created such a ferocious void in my life, such a brutal sadness, I couldn't bring myself to let him go. I pretended he was still around. All this time later, and even after the cure, sometimes I still do.

Over here. Turn around! I'm not dead.

I did turn around, convinced I would find nothing but an empty room and I would know that I was, again, going a little bit crazy. Marisa was dead like my little brother was dead, and I was hearing her voice in my head. I would hear it forever. I would never let her go. It would break my heart into tiny pieces.

"I swear he's dumber than a box of rocks."

There was nothing quite like Kate Hollander's voice to bring a person back to reality. I swung around, ran to the S3 monitor, which had never shown me anything. And there she was. Marisa was there. She was smiling, her coal black hair falling in waves around her face. I put my hand on the screen and she did the same on her end.

"What I wouldn't give to hold your hand right now," I said.

"You guys need some time alone? Because I can just go back out into the orange room of death if you do. Not a big deal, really."

"I love you," I said. "And I'm sorry."

"Oh god, I'm leaving," Kate complained. She walked straight back, away from the camera, and Marisa leaned in close.

"Ditto on the I love you part," she said. "I'm still

working on 'you're forgiven.' But we're okay. Kate wrecked the camera, but she saved the day."

I looked at her curiously, wondering what had happened, and she took the cue.

"She made a lasso out of the cord and looped it around my legs. Then she just hauled me up onto the catwalk. Kind of amazing, but there is a down side—I owe her my life."

"You could do worse!" Kate yelled from ten or so feet away.

"I have to tell you something," I said.

"Uh-oh," said Kate, who was back in a flash, eyeing me like I was about to reveal information that might ruin her life.

I was determined to stop withholding things unless I absolutely had to, but what to say, exactly, I hadn't quite figured out even as I started spilling the first part of what they didn't know.

"Rainsford is down here with us. He's Davis—you know, younger—but it's him. It's Rainsford."

Neither girl said anything for a few seconds. They stood there, stewing on this piece of information, while I prayed for Mrs. Goring not to show up on the main monitor and cut things short. I had to remember they were still getting used to the idea that Davis and Rainsford were the same person. It was fairly new information for them. Marisa was the first to speak, and her response surprised me.

"Has he got Avery with him?"

"Um, yeah. But she's . . . different."

There's a lot of talk about how girls are so competitive and catty with each other, but when push comes to shove and a bad dude is involved, never underestimate the power of girls to defend their kind.

"We have to get her away from that creep," Marisa said. "What's he done to her?"

"I think he's got her under some sort of mind control, but she's kind of listening to me, or trying to. And she looks kind of, I don't know, ghostly and more hollowed out."

"That guy is dead," said Kate, and the look on her face made me glad the two of us were on the same team.

"Wishing he was dead and getting Avery away from him are two things I'm not sure how we're going to accomplish." I was being as honest with them as I could be, but also realistic. "The guy is a lot stronger than all of us but Connor, and you know Connor is hit and miss with the dizzy spells. Rainsford's had a thousand years to learn stuff we probably don't have a clue about, like ninja skills."

"You're a geek," Kate said.

"Maybe so, but I'm serious. He's managed to lock Connor and Alex in a room and move Ben Dugan without much trouble. Maybe he's using mind tricks, but I wouldn't put hand-to-hand fighting skills out of his reach. At least there are no weapons down here."

"No one is impossible to kill," Kate said. "Not even this guy. There has to be a way to get rid of him for good."

"There is." Marisa seemed to wake up all at once from a long moment of internal thinking. "It's the vials. Mrs. Goring might be crazy, but what if she's right? What if mixing them together could erase Rainsford from the planet? We could get Avery away from him."

"And maybe get cured in the process," said Kate, which was the biggest thing she cared about. I couldn't blame her. Splitting headaches 24–7? It could make a person crazy for a cure.

"There's something else," I continued, preparing to tell them about Amy and a possible way out, at least for them. I got as far as *there's someone else . . .*

And then Mrs. Goring appeared on the central monitor, watching like she was hoping to catch me plotting something that wasn't on the approved Goring list of things to do.

"Who are you talking to?" she shouted. Wow, Bad Mood Goring was in the house. "Answer me!"

I moved close to the camera that fed the signal into the bomb shelter and leaned in so my face would fill her monitor on the other side.

"I'm talking to Kate and Marisa, who, no thanks to you, have arrived safely in the silo room. You're welcome."

Mrs. Goring's mood softened, and I realized she was probably nervous about Rainsford escaping.

"Hey, Mrs. Goring," Kate added. "Destroy any lives since we last talked?"

"Kate Hollander saves the day, how charming. I have to say though, I wasn't too concerned. I've come to expect big things from you."

Kate wasn't exactly taken aback, but her expression lightened. A compliment was a powerful weapon, even from someone who didn't care about anyone but themselves. I wanted to remind Kate that Mrs. Goring had locked us underground, put us all in extreme danger, and probably would have shrugged it off if she'd discovered that Kate and Marisa were both lying facedown in a pile of radioactive sludge.

"Can we get on with this?" I asked impatiently. "I don't want those two in there any longer than they have to be. What's the plan?"

"Look at you, getting all tough on me," Mrs. Goring said. "There may be hope for you yet, Will Besting."

A silence fell over the proceedings and I wondered what everyone else was thinking. My thoughts were split between many competing things: Rainsford, Avery, the guys all locked in a room, Amy, getting Marisa aboveground. And there was some self-pity going on, too: *Even if everyone else gets out, I'll die in this room alone. It will be lonely at the very end.*

"Both of you," said Mrs. Goring. She was straining to catch a side glimpse of Kate and Marisa in the S3 monitor, which sat against the wall to my right. "Listen very carefully. How long have you been inside that room?"

The camera was on Marisa, so I saw as she pulled out her cell phone and looked at the time. "I don't know for sure, maybe half an hour?" she said.

"It's not safe to stay in there much longer. You'll need to be clear of the area in another twenty."

"Wait, I thought you said it wasn't dangerous as long as we didn't walk on the floor?" Kate protested.

"I never said that. And even if I did, now I'm

changing my mind. Deal with it."

"Just tell us what to do, you nasty old bag."

"Warning," replied Mrs. Goring. "Objects in the S3 monitor are dumber than they appear."

"Shut up, you two!" I yelled. If I'd let them, Kate and Mrs. Goring would trade insults for half the time they had left in there without batting an eye.

"Please, Mrs. Goring, what's the plan here? Why do they need to be in there and how do I get them out?"

Mrs. Goring explained a few things about the room and the underground missile silo that we didn't previously know about. The room they were in was in fact one of the places where bombs had been stored—in the silos—and there were controls in that room for preparing them for launch. But this room wasn't where the real whopper was kept, the bomb that was big enough to fly all the way to Europe on its own power. That one had been stored in a third silo, which I was guessing was the circle on the map with the square right behind it. The other two silos, where Marisa and Kate were, contained shorter-range missiles created for strategic defense in the event of an attack.

"There were no bombs that could go that far in the 1950s," said Marisa. "I know, I sat through a cold war history semester last year."

"Don't believe everything you read, it makes you look even more foolish than you actually are."

"Okay fine, so let's assume that sixty-plus years ago we cared," Kate blasted into the conversation. "All we need to know right now is why we're in here and how to get out."

Mrs. Goring was losing patience. I knew something the girls didn't, namely that Mrs. Goring was also single-handedly preparing for a cycle of cures that would, at least she thought, make her young again. That was set to begin in a few hours. She had to be feeling the pressure.

"On the side of each silo you'll find a pair of large, round buttons. They're red, so you can't miss them. To open the door that leads inside the third silo, all four of those buttons have to be depressed at one time. I know what you're thinking—why not use duct tape, you could have done this yourself—it's not that easy."

"Why not?" I asked, thinking of the O2 marker I'd seen on the map and understanding now why I couldn't open it from inside the observation room. O2 was O zone 2, the door that would let them out.

"Because those buttons have to be pushed in a certain order, over a certain amount of time. It was designed to make sure three people would have to work together in order to give the president the ability to launch an attack."

Mrs. Goring explained that the first two buttons needed to be depressed in order, and we'd know the order because they were marked alphabetically. The A button was to be pushed in and held. After ten full seconds, within the next ten-second window, the second button was to be pushed in and held as well.

"The other two buttons are marked C and D. They're on the side of the other silo, so it needs to be a different person. When both A and B are held down, someone needs to depress the C button at the second silo sometime during the minute that follows. Once C is pressed and held, the final button should not—*must not*—be pushed for a full five minutes."

"It sounds to me like you *could* have done this with duct tape. You're just not very smart."

Kate wouldn't let up, but Mrs. Goring ignored her. She was acting like she had business of her own to attend to upstairs and was running out of patience. There was an X marker on the map at the last door, near the S4 monitor, I'd seen it. It was the door that led into the circle and the square directly behind.

"The X door will only stay unlocked for thirty seconds after D is pressed. So unless you can run back to the roof, across the catwalk, out the door, down the tunnel, and push the X door open in half a minute, I'd shut your pie hole."

Kate didn't answer, unless silently fuming as if smoke might start pouring out of her ears counted as a comeback.

"After you've pushed the last button, use the escape route I just outlined."

Mrs. Goring switched her line of sight, staring directly at me.

"Will, this is where you need to coordinate everything. Your big moment, don't screw it up."

"I appreciate the vote of confidence."

"Once that X door opens, you need to get Connor and Alex through. I have a feeling it will take both of them to finish the job."

Mrs. Goring explained that there were no cameras directly on the other side of the door, and that she wished she didn't have to send two Neanderthals with less than half a brain between them.

"That silo is flooded with water, so they'll need to swim across. I know what you're thinking , but it's okay. It's clear of any electrical charge, I guarantee it. Once you get them that far, we'll have contact again."

A Goring guarantee, how comforting. But it rang true—she wouldn't put us through all these hoops just to fry us in the end.

I was turned around, looking at the map on the wall, and understood right away what she was talking about.

"The S5 station, inside the room behind the circle."

"You guessed it."

"So that's where the vials are kept?" Marisa asked as she, too, strained to see the map from where she stood.

"Yes, that's where the vials are kept," said Mrs. Goring.

"It's a three-person job. How'd our vials get in there to begin with?"

It was a reasonable question to ask, no doubt.

"Rainsford, that little ogre Avery, and your doctor."

"Wait, you mean Dr. Stevens helped lock this stuff away, even after she knew what really went on here?"

"Stupid boy. What makes you think she didn't *always* know? Rainsford has a way with his offspring that is quite, shall we say, *persuasive*. Half the time she doesn't know *what* she's doing."

"You live in a twisted family, mommy dearest," Kate said.

Kate's comment seemed to dig at the core of who Mrs. Goring was, a mother who'd badly failed her child. She started to fume, like she was going to say something, but she seemed to think better of it. Maybe she was harnessing that particular kind of anger so she could use it against Rainsford instead. She reached up and turned her monitor off.

"Now you've gone and chased her away," Marisa said with a slight smile on her face.

"Yeah, big bummer. Will? Have you thought about how Rainsford and Avery might complicate this little plan?"

"And how we can't be in here for more than about fifteen more minutes?" Marisa asked.

"I've been thinking a lot about both of those things. You guys figure out where the knobs are, I'll get to work. I'll be back in ten minutes or less."

"You better be," Kate said.

"And Will? Go easy on Avery. She's one of us. Let's get her back."

That last part was less a plea than a challenge from Marisa. She, more than anyone else, was concerned about Avery and the mess she'd gotten herself into. I appreciated this about Marisa, the way she zeroed in on what really mattered. This was about us, *all of us*, getting out alive. Oddly enough, it was Avery I would need to lean on if I had any chance of getting the X door open and the right people on the other side.

And I needed her for something even bigger, something no one else had thought about, or so it seemed. It was funny how Mrs. Goring dropped small clues in the things she said. She must have known I'd think of it eventually.

Mrs. Goring was a seventh. She carried her vial with her. And we needed all seven of our vials in order for the mixture to work.

That seventh vial wouldn't be in the room behind the door marked with an X.

No, the seventh vial was carried by the seventh person cured.

Avery was turning out to be more important than I'd imagined she could be. Without her there was no cure for us and no poison for Rainsford.

Without Avery there was nothing.

6:30 PM — 7:00 PM

"Avery, listen to me," I said, seeing her sitting cold and alone at the S1 station. She hadn't moved since I'd last seen her, and she looked exactly the same: a ghostly figure, half alive and half dead. Her head tilted up toward me, and I wondered how long it had been since she'd eaten anything.

"You were one of us once, remember that?" I started. She had no response, so I continued on.

"We all showed up at Fort Eden for the same reason—

to get cured. But we were lied to, Avery. You and all the rest of us, we were fed a steady diet of lies for years before we even got there. And I've got some bad news for you. She's doing it again. Mrs. Goring has a whole new set of seven people up there, and starting tonight, she's going to repeat the procedure. Only this time, she's doing it on herself. We can't let that happen."

Something about what I'd said got Avery's attention. She was up on her feet, more alive than dead, staring at me like a phantom that had decided there was still work to be done on this side of the grave.

"She's trying to get him back," Avery said. "She'll take him from me."

"No, no . . ." Wow, not the answer I was expecting, but in a twisted way there was some logic to it. "She hates Rainsford more than anyone. You said it yourself—she tried to kill him more than once—she just wants to . . ."

And there I was stuck. Mrs. Goring was hell-bent on killing the guy Avery loved, not stealing him away. What could I say that would make Avery want to help me? At least part of the truth contained the destruction of Rainsford, a young version with whom Avery was madly in love. I stuck with the facts that had a sliver of a chance of helping.

"Goring sent us down here to get seven vials of blood, blood that came out of our cures. We mix all that blood together, and it's a cure for the things they took from us. Even if you don't want to be cured, we do. And remember one thing—you ended up with white hair, we got it a lot worse. Our ailments have real consequences."

"Tell me the truth, Will. You're lying," Avery said. She was wearing a black T-shirt and jeans, and one of her hands had drifted into a pocket.

She has it. She has her vial, I thought.

"No! I'm not lying to you, seriously."

"But you're not telling me everything."

I looked at my watch—three minutes already gone—and decided to go for broke.

"If we mix the vials together, the mixture will cure us. But it will *kill* her. It will kill Eve Goring."

This got Avery's attention. She was so interesting to watch, because part of her seemed lucid, normal. But another part was detached and troubled, like she might snap at any moment.

"How do you know that?"

"Dr. Stevens told me. She hates Goring."

More deceit off the top of my head. I was getting almost too good at this.

"Are you lying to me, Will Besting?"

I was, totally. But Avery was halfway to believing me, not because it rang true, but because she needed the rules of the world to be this way. She needed to believe there was a secret way of killing her competition.

"No, it's the truth. I'm telling you the truth. And I know you love Davis or Rainsford or whoever this guy is at this particular moment in history, but just hear me out on this. He dumped his old age into us. He betrayed us. And in the end, there is no evidence to support the idea that he won't abandon you when having you around isn't to his liking anymore. Avery, I'm sorry, but Rainsford is a heartless bastard. He just is."

Avery stared straight into my eyes, and for the glimmer of a moment I could see that she knew I might be right. I'd broken through, briefly but importantly, and I knew somewhere inside all that hollowed-out skin lived the girl I once knew.

"Power of love, Will," Avery said in her haunted voice. "It's timeless and immortal, you know?"

"Yeah, I know. I really do."

I was thinking of Marisa and how it wouldn't matter if we were separated by death. I'd love her always, to the end of time.

"Open the door, I'll get you the vials."

"How?"

"Just do it, Will. I'll get them."

I was lower than low on options. I had to get someone past that X door in five minutes or less no matter what. I'd given her my best arguments.

"Help us, Avery. We need you."

And with that I pushed the control for the red zone door, opening it.

"There's a door marked X down there. You know about that door?"

"Of course I know. Davis told me."

"And you know what's in there?"

Avery didn't answer, but she did turn in my direction and stare, as if I was being ridiculous. Of course she knew.

"We need our vials. It's that simple."

She started to walk away without responding, then turned back.

"Leave it open."

"What? Why?"

"Just do as I say. Leave it open."

She didn't say anything else, just moved down the tunnel, through the door, and out of my line of sight.

Maybe she had bigger plans than I could hope for, like retrieving all my friends and sending them out of the red zone. I fired up the S4 monitor, where I'd left Rainsford waiting for almost an hour. I expected to find him standing there, ready to kill one of my friends for locking Avery on my side of a door he couldn't get through, but of course he was gone. There was no one. It was as if the red zone was deserted, had in fact never been inhabited to begin with. It was all just a bad dream I was going to wake up from.

I opened up the S3 feed, where Kate and Marisa were, and saw that they had found the buttons. They were waiting impatiently for me to fire the start gun.

I calculated the time and figured I could wait maybe three more minutes. If I started them then, they'd be stuck holding down knobs for five more, then they'd have to get out fast through the number-two O zone door. I took one more look at the map, holding the green key card in my hand, and thinking about when I would try to use it.

Not yet. Maybe not ever. It won't work anyway.

Getting out of the silo room would be fast, just a few minutes. It would have to be close enough. It was the best I could do.

"Who are you going to trust, me or her?"

I spun around on my heels so fast I nearly fell over. I knew that voice and went first to where I expected it had come from—a lightning-fast glance at S4, where I'd last seen Rainsford. But he wasn't there. No, he'd moved. He was much closer now.

He was at S1, just down the tunnel from me. He'd taken Avery's place.

In a flash I slammed the red zone lockdown control, and the room filled with an echoing buzz.

"That door won't close until I take the metal bar out. I blocked it, Will. It's not rocket science."

The blaring was constant and loud, and I could hear Kate and Marisa yelling in the background, wondering what was happening in my small neck of the woods.

I turned the S1 monitor off and stared at Marisa, who looked wide-eyed and afraid.

"Now! Do it now, Marisa!"

Marisa ran away from the monitor, pushing Kate in front of her until they were both out of sight. I hoped they'd devised some way of counting down the time so they'd get it right.

"Can you hear me?" I shouted, but there was no reply. Either they were too far away or my hearing was bad enough I couldn't make out their voices.

I looked quickly at the S4 monitor and saw no one. My only hope was to keep Rainsford occupied long enough that Avery could get Connor and Alex free. But would she even do it? Would she play along? It was starting to feel like I'd been tricked into letting her out and Rainsford in.

I was just taking a deep breath to steady my nerves before turning Rainsford's station back on, when I heard a loud pounding on the metal door.

It was him: Rainsford, standing outside, trying to force his way through. For once I was happy the door was firmly locked. The pounding stopped as fast as it had started and I watched the main monitor as Rainsford crossed through the entryway section on his way back to S1. By the time he got there, I had turned the monitor back on and the blaring sound of alert had stopped.

"Did you hear what I asked you?" he began. "Who are you going to trust, me or her?"

"I don't even know what you're talking about."

"Sure you do, Will. You're a smart kid. It's why Eve chose you."

"You mean Mrs. Goring?"

"She's Eve to me, always will be. But she's also out of

her mind. She tried to kill me. You think she won't try to kill you, too? Think again."

"What did you do with my friends?"

"Friends? Please, Will, let's at least be honest about what those people mean to you. They aren't your friends. You only care about one person down here, and that's Marisa Sorrento. You should be thanking me. I led you to her."

"The hell you did. Where's Connor? Where's Alex and Ben?"

He wouldn't answer me.

"You shouldn't try to turn Avery against me. She doesn't understand what I'm capable of. Better that way, know what I mean?"

I hated Rainsford so much it was hard not lashing out at him. So smug, so full of the world and all it had to offer. He'd had it all, ten times over. He'd outlive me, then do it all over again. He'd outlive the kids I hadn't even had yet.

"You tricked Avery. You tricked all of us."

"True. But I cured you, too. It's a problem with your generation. You don't appreciate anything. Always focused on the negative."

I was talking, but I was also calculating. By now Kate

would be pressing the D button. I couldn't turn on S4 without turning Rainsford off for fear of what he might see, and I was afraid turning off his monitor would set him to thinking. *What's going on back at the ranch? Could Avery be deceiving me?*

All I could do was hope Avery had freed Connor, Alex, and Ben and pointed them in the direction of a door marked with an X.

"You're the only one," Rainsford said. "Did you know that?"

"You mean the only person who knows the truth? You're wrong about that."

"No, you don't understand. Lots of people have known, down through the many years. I've told people. I told Avery and Eve. It just slips out, you know? A hard secret to keep. But they don't really remember, not like you remember. I'm always sure to maintain control."

"How long have you been alive?" I asked, a bold question I expected no answer to.

"Longer than you think, and I'm betting you think I've been around awhile."

"A thousand years?"

He glanced back toward the red zone door and seemed to forget something, then looked toward the O zone.

"I heard a voice before. You were talking to someone. Is she down here? This way? I bet she is."

Rainsford was staring down the hall, in the direction of the blue zone, after which came the door to the room filled with glowing orange dust. The room that could kill you all by itself. And he had something in his hand, which he started waving in front of me.

It was a key card and it was blue.

"Funny the things you find in a missile silo supply room, isn't it? Stuff just lying around with no purpose. It gets boring in a room like that with nothing to do but search through old boxes."

I was speechless. He had a key card, a blue one. He could open that door. A monster with no soul, no heart, was close enough to Marisa to get hold of her. On top of that I was in a panic at the thought of what was going on at S4, if the guys were out or if Avery was against me. But it didn't matter what I thought or how I felt. None of it mattered as Amy came up on the main monitor, the mystery girl from upstairs, staring at me as I tried to shake my head.

No. Don't speak. Don't give yourself away.

"You can't change the way Avery feels," Rainsford said. "So do me a favor and stop trying. She'll do as she's told. They all do."

Rainsford walked away in the direction of the blue zone, but not before giving me a look that said everything he needed me to know.

You made a mistake trying to turn her against me. I won't stand for that. I think I'll teach you a lesson by walking down here and killing your girlfriend.

Amy had a curious look on her face. She'd heard the voice, a person she didn't know and couldn't understand. The very idea of explaining the myriad connections to someone who didn't know any of what I was dealing with sent a wave of anger through me. Not so much *at* Amy but at the crazy, swirling events of the past few hours that made her so oblivious.

"Who was that?"

I couldn't even answer her without my voice filling with sarcasm.

"A guy you don't want to meet but somehow I think you will and when you do he'll charm you and make you believe his lies and he'll ruin your life and you'll become a zombie and you'll betray all you know and follow him into the abyss and he will never, ever end—but you, Amy—you will end, as sure as I'm standing here, you will definitely come to an end."

Wow. Did I just say that? I thought. *I guess I did.*

Amy had struck me as a simple girl from the start, but there was something about her that lacked the sadness or the weariness of having feared with total desperation. It suddenly made me nervous even talking to her.

"Sorry I asked," she said. "And also I came down here to tell you that Mrs. Goring pushed the cure to later tonight. She wants it to be dark outside, I don't know why. Maybe she's spending all her time dealing with *you* instead, or whatever. Anyway, if you still want me to, I can go open that thing up right after we eat, so like an hour from now. You want me to or not?"

I had wondered, as Amy talked, where Rainsford was. By now he would have passed by the entryway camera and found his way to the blue zone door. If only he didn't have that key card! I could have stopped worrying about how far he'd gone. He'd have found the door locked and given up.

But watching the S2 camera, I knew that was not to be. It was sad, really, to think of them holding down those buttons while this beast of a human being got closer and closer. Nowhere to run, nowhere to hide.

"I'll see you soon, everything will be better then," Amy said. "You'll see."

Amy must have been upset that I was ignoring her

and acting like a jerk, because she cut the feed from the bomb shelter a second later after a wistful smile that faded into an empty view of the entry to the missile silo.

I cycled on the S4 station—nothing—then held the green key card in hand, knowing that if ever there was a time to use it, the moment was now.

Five minutes were up. Marisa and Kate would be coming out of the silo room, moving up onto the catwalk, and heading for the door on the far end of the O zone.

I stepped to the broken card reader, hanging like a killed animal against the wall, and held it in my right hand.

One shot. Please, just open the door.

I slid the green card against the circuit board, along the line of pale light that would either activate the door lock or blow the fuse.

There was a crack like lightning, an electrical charge up my forearm, and a flickering of the lights. I was blown back onto the floor, the charred green key card no longer in my hand.

When I looked up, the card reader was hissing smoke. And there was something else, something far more important.

The door to the observation room was open.

7:00 PM—8:00 PM

7:00 PM — 7:30 PM

It should have felt good, even a little bit exciting. I'd been trapped in the observation room all alone for hours, and now the door stood open. I could get up off the floor and leave without anyone stopping me. The fact that I wanted to stay made me wonder what sort of person I'd become.

What's wrong with you, bro? This is the part where you run out the door and save the day!

I'm not good at that kind of thing, Keith. You should know that by now.

You're just feeling sorry for yourself. Get up off your ass and show Rainsford what you're made of.

But it wasn't that I felt sorry for myself. My little brother didn't understand me in death any better than he had when he was alive. Or maybe I'm just complicated. There were reasons I stayed on the floor, and none of them had anything to do with feeling sorry for myself. Exiting the observation room meant leaving the comfort of the monitors. I'd lose my ability to observe what was going on. It had been my keen advantage all along and it was risky giving it up, even for a few minutes. Plus Mrs. Goring could show up while I was away. Finding me not there, I had to assume, would not make her happy. It would complicate her motives even more and possibly increase the chances of her leaving us underground forever. But most of all, I was afraid of Rainsford. There, I said it. Sure I hated the guy and knew he deserved to die ten times over. But he was angry, indestructible, and bigger than me. How was I *supposed* to feel?

I stayed on my back until a larger, more important thought cast a black shadow over everything. I couldn't let Rainsford anywhere near Marisa. I'd go down fighting to save her even if she never knew I'd done it.

I got up on my feet and took one last look at all the

monitors, catching sight of two or three shadowy figures on S4. They were in the tunnel and then they weren't, and I knew Avery had gotten at least one person out of the room. They vanished from the screen, heading for the door marked X and the secret places that lay beyond.

I stepped out into the hall and pulled the door to the observation room most of the way shut and ran toward the red zone. The lights crackled and fizzed over my head as drops of water fell from the rusted metal ceiling. Feeling the water made me realize how thirsty I was as I came to the corner and turned right. I was in a dead sprint for the door when it swung open unexpectedly.

Ben Dugan, who had hobbled all the way back through the red zone, jumped back at the sight of me.

"Will? You got out!"

"Get in here! Quick, I gotta move," I demanded, pulling Ben through the opening without thinking of his injuries. He flinched with pain.

"Take it easy. My back's killing me."

"But you're fine, right? You're okay?"

"Yeah, like you said before—banged up is all. I'll live. I'm better than Avery, that's for sure. She looks like the walking dead. Scared me half to death when she opened the door and let us out."

Ben wouldn't shut up. He kept going on and on about her hair and her skin and how the room was cold and full of all sorts of junk. I tuned him out, picked up the metal pipe Rainsford had used to block the opening, and slammed the red zone door shut.

"Listen to me Ben, this is important. Get to the green room, where I was. *Do not* shut the door behind you, keep it barely open so it looks like it's shut."

I was already walking rapidly away, leaving him behind as he tried to talk and I kept on giving instructions.

"When you get in there lie down under the long control panel—you'll see it—and no matter what, don't talk to anyone but me. If you hear other voices, don't respond. You got it?"

"Yeah, I got it. Where are you going?"

"Just go, Ben! As fast as you can get there. And wait for me. It won't be too long."

I didn't look back as Ben kept talking and talking. He was in a chatty mood at the worst possible time, and I wished he'd shut up so I could concentrate on what I was doing. The metal pipe was about three feet long and solid. I felt stronger and safer carrying it with me, like I might have a fighting chance. I passed through the entryway with the hole that led up and out of the underground, hoping Mrs. Goring hadn't been watching. The blue door was next, and as I'd suspected, Rainsford had left it wide open so he could return if he wanted to. How many minutes did he have on me? Five? Ten? I couldn't be sure as I came to the first of two sections of flooring that had broken away. They were bigger openings than I'd expected and they threatened to slow me down, but I took the first one at a run and leaped across, a crazy idea because it was about seven feet to the other side. I hadn't long-jumped, but Keith had done it in middle school and gone over fourteen feet. I was sure I could make half that far.

And I did. Only the tile I landed on didn't hold. It fell free into the mucky water below as my forward momentum carried me onto my knees. I was racked with an electrical charge from the splash of water. My teeth locked down against the fat part of my tongue and I tasted warm blood in my mouth. Pain shot through my knees as they crashed into the hard tile floor, and I slid uncontrollably forward. When the electricity floated cleanly out of my body, I was staring at the second hole, where Kate and Marisa had helped each other across. I'd let go of the metal pipe and it was rolling away. I leapt forward, banging my elbows on the hard floor, lying flat out against

209

the tiles, my fingers grasping the only weapon I had just as it was about to fall into the second hole. My fingers curled around the pipe and I stood up.

Time's running out, I thought. Rainsford was probably on the catwalk by then, a catwalk that Kate and Marisa were also going to use. I felt my tongue swelling inside my mouth and the lingering feeling that I'd just been filled with an electric charge. A few inches shorter on that jump and I'd have been finished.

The second hole was longer, and staring at it I knew it would be impossible for me to clear if I tried to jump. I took the side Kate had taken, slowly making my way along the rounded edge of the tunnel as I listened for any sign of life up ahead. It took valuable time I didn't have, but finally I cleared the second electrified pool of water and ran for the O zone. That door stood open, too, and staring inside I was momentarily stunned by the brightness of the orange floor. It was menacing, disturbing, beautiful. Like a perfect sea of warm sand on a cool day, it begged to be walked on. So still, so treacherous. I could feel its deadly power waiting to be unleashed.

I pulled the O zone door shut behind me, stepping on the ladder to my left as I did so, and I heard the sucking sound of the room being sealed off from the rest of the world. This was not a door that would lock from the observation room, that much I'd already figured out on my own. And the O zone door on the far end of the room? It, too, was not a door I knew how to lock.

Rising quickly on the rungs, I moved with as much stealth as I could while holding a three-foot metal pipe in one hand, until I stood on the flimsy catwalk. It was harrowing to look at, and I found myself feeling utterly amazed that Kate and Marisa had willingly made their way across. I could see, down the way, where the catwalk had fallen through and hung in sheets of metal. One false move and the section could fall into the glowing orange floor. It would send a plume of radioactive dust high into the air. It would eviscerate every living thing in the room.

But none of those unbelievably hazardous elements had my attention. Not the faulty catwalk or the hanging sections of metal grating or the orange floor of death. They all fell away in comparison to the girl in the distance and the man who stood between us.

"Will Besting, you never cease to amaze me," said Rainsford. He smiled at me and a leftover tremor of electricity ran down my spine and into my guts. I hated him, feared him, loathed him.

"Marisa!" I yelled. Kate was standing behind her, farther away. "Get down the ladder on that side! There's a door. You can make it!"

"Yes, by all means!" Rainsford agreed. He stood sideways, glancing back and forth between Marisa and Kate and me. "It's Will you need to worry about, not me. I can get you the vials. All he's going to do is get you into more trouble."

"Leave him alone!" yelled Marisa. Kate was unusually quiet, like she was having trouble deciding what to do and talking would only confuse her more.

"Wait for me on the other side and I'll make sure you find those vials," said Rainsford. "Let Will and me do some catching up."

I had been slowly walking toward Rainsford while he spoke and arrived within a few paces of where he stood. The railing at the side of the wide catwalk was loose and unsteady. Every step I took fell on another wobbly section of grating. The whole thing felt like a house of cards that could collapse at any moment. It was for that reason that I screamed when Rainsford crouched down and began deliberately forcing the catwalk into a wave of movement beneath my feet. Kate and Marisa screamed, too, but Rainsford laughed.

"Oh come on, isn't it thrilling the way it moves? It's like the fun house at the fair!"

Kate decided she'd had enough and started down the ladder on the far side, coaxing Marisa to go with her. I wished Marisa could bring herself to leave me behind, but she couldn't. In fact she started walking toward me with determination, the last thing I wanted her to do.

"Marisa, no!"

But it turned out to be exactly what I needed. Rainsford was so captivated by the idea that Marisa would come for me—that she would willingly choose death in order to try and save me—he turned fully in her direction and stared in awe.

When he did, I took two fast steps toward him and swung the metal pipe. It caught Rainsford on the side of the head and he reeled back, waving his arms drunkenly. He stood straight up again, shook his head four or five times, and seemed to recover. I swung again, this time toward his midsection, and connected with a deadly thud that buckled him over. Sliding the pipe out, I raised it over my head, aiming for what I hoped would be a final blow against his back.

Time slowed down, nearly stopped. I saw Marisa's wide eyes fill with the horror of watching me kill a man.

I saw the door on the other side of the room swing open, watched Kate start through and turn back, waiting for us. I felt the catwalk begin to buckle in ways that felt more troubling than before. And then I went into a sort of stupor as Rainsford stood bolt upright so very fast. I tried to swing down with the pipe but he caught its middle in one hand, ripping it free in one clean motion. He smiled wickedly at me as blood flowed down the side of his head and neck.

"You'll have to do better then that, Will Besting."

Rainsford started to move toward me, a surprising steadiness in his steps. He dropped the pipe, presumably because he didn't think he'd need it to finish off such a little guy like me, and the pipe rolled dangerously close to the edge of the catwalk.

He didn't see Marisa behind him, sucking in a huge breath and holding it. I did the same just as she pushed Rainsford with all her might, grabbed my hand, and began to run. I reached down, grabbing the metal pipe before it could fall into the sea of orange below, and kept running.

I couldn't help looking back, even though it wasn't very smart. I could have tripped and fallen so easily. But Marisa's hand was firmly wrapped around mine, where it belonged, and I just had to see.

He had broken through the railing; free falling, back to the floor, staring up at me. His eyes told me that even he wondered if his immortality could withstand an attack like the one he was about to encounter. But more than that, his confidence carried him. He'd lived in the world too long for his imagination to include a killing machine with the power to take him out. I could read his mind in those eyes of his.

This will be interesting. But make no mistake, it won't undo me. You watch.

We were ten long strides from the ladder on the far side of the open room when Rainsford hit. It was one of the strangest things I'd ever seen. I had expected to see a burst of orange dust fill the room, dust that if it caught me would surely kill me on contact. But a hundred seventy-five pounds of humanity hitting a fifty-year-old pile of radioactive waste turned out to be more like hitting a rolling floor of toxic Jell-O. The whole floor moved like a slow, soft ocean. It was boiling up in waves, releasing pockets of gas and dust in a million different places at once. Rainsford's weight seemed to push the floor in at the point of impact, like a bubble being forced to the breaking point, sloshing and pumping every part of a living creature. By the time we reached the ladder I knew we were in trouble.

The bubble finally burst. Rainsford's weight ripped a hole in the orange mass, and from that hole came the violent burst of radiant ash as if a volcano had just erupted from the floor of the vast room. Marisa literally dove through the air in the direction of the door, landing in Kate's arms as the two of them tumbled in a pile beyond where I could see them. I felt the hot wind of death coming my way and saw the explosion of dust sweeping toward me. If I didn't reach the door, get through it, and shut it in time, I wouldn't be the only one who would suffer the force of what we'd unleashed. Everyone underground would come to an end. We'd all die.

All but one.

I knew this beyond a shadow of a doubt for one simple reason. As I leapt through the opening and grabbed the door by its thick iron handle, I heard a final noise. Right before the slamming of the door and the vacuum seal sound of sucking.

The last thing I heard coming from inside the room was the sound of Rainsford laughing.

7:30 PM — 8:00 PM

I stood vacantly, looking down at Marissa. She wasn't moving. I had come to know this habit about her, this way of being, too well; so well that, at first, her stillness didn't alarm me as it should have. She was a girl who liked to sleep and she was good at it. I'd turned to my left or my right a thousand times and found her dozed off, the warmth of slumber filling every part of her. She is a remarkably attractive sleeper, which can't be said of all people, including myself. Marisa is soft when she sleeps.

If we're sitting on a couch she will pull me around her like a blanket and fall away into a cup-shaped form, our bodies held together by dreams and whispers.

"Snap out of it, Will! Hey, you in there!"

"Wake up, man!"

Kate was slapping me hard on the shoulder, rousing me back to reality. And was that . . . *Connor*?

"Did you breathe any of it into your lungs? Did you?!"

"I—I don't know," I stammered, staring down at Marisa, who was lying on her side. "What's wrong with her? Is she okay?"

"She's fine, Will—just exhausted. I think the stress is getting to her even more than usual."

Kate was at my hand, trying to wrench something free I wasn't willing to let go of. Connor just stood there, gaping at us all, like he didn't know what to do.

"Give it to me, Will. Just let it go. I need to bar this door so he can't get out."

"What?" I looked in my own hand and found that I'd carried the metal pipe all the way out of the O zone with me. I don't know why I did it or even how, but there it was, still in my grasp as I held it out and loosened my grip.

"I heard him laughing," said Kate, shaking her head like she couldn't even begin to believe it. "At least let's make sure he doesn't get out if we can help it."

"She told me to guard the door," said Connor, "I should go back."

"Guard what door? And who? What are you talking about?" Kate asked.

Connor pointed down the rusted, dripping tunnel.

"Avery—who by the way looks pretty bad if you ask me—she and Alex went in, but I was supposed to guard the door. Make sure Davis couldn't get in. Or Rainsford, whatever this dude's name is."

Like you could stop him if you tried, I thought.

"Just go, yeah—wait for us there," Kate said impatiently. She went to the O zone door and Connor took off in the other direction. Looking down at Marisa, I got the feeling she was waking up. Was this her new reality? Like a narcoleptic, would she simply go to sleep at the most inopportune times? I leaned down over her, pushing her dark hair back and feeling her skin. It was warm as I'd hoped, and her hand came up to mine. Her cheek was soft against my hand, her palm against my fingers like a butterfly perched and ready to fly.

"You scared me," I said.

"You scared me, too. Let's try not to do that to each other anymore, okay?"

Her eyes opened and I saw that she was smiling. She reached up, took my shirt in her hand, and pulled me close.

Let's just say it was the best kiss of my life up to that point. Five seconds, ten? I couldn't say, but somewhere in that general time frame my eyes came fully open. I'd remembered something important.

"Shut the blue door," I said, not nearly loud enough. Then I was up, moving as fast as my feet would carry me to the S4 monitor. "Ben! Lock the blue door!"

I was yelling into the screen, hoping I hadn't been too late, wondering if Ben Dugan was in the observation room waiting for me to give him instructions. There was a long, stress-inducing silence as I stared into an empty room but got no reply.

"What's going on?" asked Kate. She'd returned from her chore at the O zone door.

"The other O zone entry, it doesn't lock either," I said as Marisa got up and came over, too. The three of us stared into the monitor. "I left the blue door open and put Ben in the observation room. If he doesn't get that door shut, Rainsford could get out."

"Is the observation room locked?" asked Marisa. "If it's not it should be."

"Ben!" I yelled. "Come out, let me know you're okay."

I had a chilling sense that Rainsford was about to pop his orange-covered head into the monitor and hold up Ben's dead body. I'd tried to kill Rainsford. He would be furious.

"Hang on, I'm coming. Give me a second."

"Hey, that's him—that's Ben. I know that voice," said Marisa. "Ben!"

"You need to lock the blue zone right now!" I yelled.

Ben came into view, slowly and with some effort, and I saw that he wasn't doing as well as I'd hoped.

"My back is seizing up on me—couldn't get up off the floor."

"Oh, Ben—I'm sorry," said Marisa. "Is the door locked? Close it so no one can get in."

"No, wait!" I countered. "There's no key card. It's fried, trust me. If you lock that door you won't be able to get out, maybe ever. Just engage the blue lock, Ben. He can't be past there yet."

"Whoa."

"Wait, what? What's going on?" I asked. Ben looked like he'd just seen a ghost but couldn't get his legs to move and run away.

"It's Rainsford," said Ben, mesmerized by something

I couldn't see but he could. "Dude, he just walked right into one of those holes with the electric water."

"This is bad," said Kate.

"Ben, hit the blue button! Do it now, before he gets to the door."

"You don't understand," Ben said, squinting his eyes and leaning closer to the wall of monitors. "He's lying down in the water. He's gone."

"Gone? What do you mean, gone?" Kate asked.

"Okay, he's moving fast, like *really* fast," Ben said. "But he's under the water. This is weird, you guys. The tunnel is filled with sparks. The guy is, I don't know— I think he's washing something off himself. How's that even possible?"

Rainsford was taking a bath in a high-voltage pool of age-old water, an act that would kill a mortal in no time flat. He was clearing his system of whatever gunk Marisa had pushed him into. All the procedures over all those years really had made him unkillable. He was Rainsford, the immortal. He couldn't be stopped.

"Which button do I push again?" Ben asked, glancing down at a console I'd become all too familiar with.

"Blue, round, big."

"Um . . . yeah. I see it."

"Hit it!" I yelled. Marisa and Kate yelled, too, and Ben looked at the monitor with Rainsford on it and his eyes widened. He hit the button hard and fast, then stepped back from the control panel.

There was a long silence, maybe five seconds straight, where no one spoke. I looked at Ben and raised my eyebrows.

Did you get the door locked in time?

He nodded, yes, and I felt a little better. At least Rainsford was contained for the moment. I was actually feeling pretty good, like it was all a big game and we'd surged into a position where we might actually win.

And then the truth struck me. What was I, a total moron?

Rainsford had a blue key card.

He could open the door anytime he wanted to.

"Ben, what's he doing now?" I asked as calmly as I could.

"He's still in the water, but he's sitting up now. The dude is like Frankenstein."

"Which pool is he in? The one close to the monitor or the one down at the end, by the blue door?"

"The one by the monitor. He seems to be taking his time."

"Good, hang on—and don't shut that green door. Also, get down and stay quiet. If Goring shows up, she can't know you're in there. Only talk to *me*, got it?"

"Got it, and I'm more than happy to lie down. I don't feel so good."

Ben slid slowly out of view, and I knew I had very little time. I had to take complete command of the situation, and fast. It was risky what I was doing. I was taking Ben's life in my own hands. I was the only one who knew Rainsford had a blue key card. Only I knew that Rainsford could get to Ben Dugan. The question was whether or not I could make it to the blue door first.

"Marisa, you and Kate stay with Connor," I said, backpedaling toward the O zone door as Kate followed me. "Wait for Avery and Alex to come out. And find a weapon if you can—anything—I don't know if Avery can be trusted."

Marisa nodded, asked me where I was going.

"Just trust me, okay? Can you do that?"

Marisa nodded again. I'd won back her confidence and I aimed to do everything I could to keep it that way. Seconds later I arrived at the O zone door with Kate. She'd figured out the perfect way to slide the bar through the opening on the handle and jam the edge into the corner by the door.

"I need to take that bar with me," I said. "He's not going to come this way. It's too far, and he knows he'd drag all that radioactive garbage along with him. He's clearing his system so he can be with Avery, right? He's only going to go the other way."

Kate wanted to protest, I could see it in her eyes. But she'd heard everything, knew what was going on in the blue zone. She knew Rainsford was making a break in the other direction.

"He can get out, can't he?" she asked, searching my eyes for the truth.

I popped the bar out of its position and slid it free of the O zone door.

"I hope not" was the best I could do.

I instructed Kate to stay at the monitor so I could communicate if I made it back to the observation room and I told her where Marisa and Connor were stationed. Then I raced through the tunnel until I reached the opening that led to the X door. Connor and Marisa stood there, shadowy in the soft light.

"Stay here," I instructed. "Kate's at the monitor—she'll alert you when I call. If anything interesting happens, go tell her. I should be online in ten minutes, hopefully less."

"Be careful," Marisa said.

"I'll take care of the girls, no worries," Connor added. I wanted to mention that he hadn't been very useful so far, but I let it pass and hoped he could at least help guide everyone out of the red zone when the time came.

And then I was off, making my way as fast as I could past holes in the floor, each time trying to imagine what Rainsford was doing. How long did it take to wash radioactive sludge off your skin when you were using high-voltage liquid? I doubted even Rainsford knew, though probably he could feel how long it would take. I rounded the first of two corners in the red zone and remembered something very important.

"Kate!" I screamed, my voice bouncing wildly through the tunnel system. She was a long way off, far enough that I couldn't see her in the gloom, but she answered. My hearing was a problem, as always, and whatever she said came through like the sound of a hamster squeaking into a tin can. At least she'd caught my voice.

"Tell Ben to open the red zone door!" I screamed. It wouldn't do me much good to arrive at the door and find it locked tight. I yelled once more for good measure as loud as my voice would go, *"Open the red door!"*

Did she hear me and understand? Would Ben be able

to get up off the floor in the observation room and do what she asked? Had Mrs. Goring appeared in the room, looking for me? All questions I asked myself as I kept on, arriving at the two remaining holes in the floor. They were both long but narrow, easy to get around but menacing to look at. They were filled with shards of tile and thick, exposed tubes of wire that snaked over and under the water's surface. The tubes looked like serpents that might reach out and wrap themselves around my legs at any moment, sucking me under as Rainsford had gone under. Only I'd die and he wouldn't. The unfairness of it all seized in my mind, a fuel of anger and fear and regret for allowing myself to be tricked again.

Fool me once, right bro?

Yeah, I know the saying, Keith. I don't need to hear it.

It's a good one, though, right? Fool me once, shame on you. Fool me twice, shame on me.

Shut up, Keith. You're bugging me.

You always had a way of getting us out of a jam though, right? It was your specialty.

It was rare for Keith's voice to rear up in my mind in the past tense, so it caught me off guard.

You always had a way of getting us out of a jam though, right? It was your specialty.

Past tense had a different kind of power. I had to face the fact of losing him all over again, the knowing he was gone.

As I came to the red zone door I pushed my little brother's voice deep down inside. I couldn't tell if the door was open or shut, and part of me didn't know which result I hoped to find. Past the door was now Rainsford's realm. I'd hit him in the side of the head with the metal pipe I was carrying. He'd want revenge. If he'd cleared the blue zone I was history, me and Ben both.

How long had it been since I'd last seen Rainsford taking a high-voltage dip? Ten minutes? Longer? Time was warped in my head in a way that made it feel more like ten hours had already gone by and I was about to open a door and find a monster standing behind it.

I touched the red zone door, slick and metallic, and pushed. It was heavy like the others and moved slowly. On the other side it was very dark, only a single soft bulb to light thirty or more feet of tunnel.

A figure stood in the distance, bathed in blue light from a monitor on the wall. He'd come for me, probably already stopped over in the observation room and killed Ben Dugan. And the red door was open, too. He could have his pick of victims: Connor, Alex, Kate, Marisa.

They wouldn't have a chance.

"That you, Will?"

It was not the voice I'd expected.

"Ben?"

"Yeah, it's me. I got scared in there. And it feels better if I move around some, doesn't seize up on me."

I ran through the door toward Ben's silhouette.

"Whoa, what's the rush? Take it easy, he's behind the blue door, remember?"

"Start running! Get through the red door!" I yelled. Ben needed to be safe and away from the observation room. I didn't even stop at the turn where Ben stood, I just blew past him and kept on going, yelling for him to get back in the red zone as fast as he possibly could.

"Why would I want to do that? It's cold in there, plus—"

"Go, Ben! Just go right now! It's not safe here! And shut the door behind you!"

I was screaming the words over my head as I passed under the hole with the ladder that led up to the surface. I wondered if Amy would unlock the latch and let us all out. There was still a chance I could find a way to escape, to free everyone.

I rounded the last corner, sliding and falling on the

slick tile floor. When my shoulder hit, the tiles broke through, revealing a river of water below through two feet of empty space. I scrambled to my feet, barely avoiding disaster, and came to the blue door. It was closed, thank God, but it wouldn't stay that way for long. The card reader on my side of the door had a soft blue light about the size of a pencil eraser. It was flashing and beeping. There was a loud click and the light went solid again.

The door had been unlocked from the other side.

I grabbed the handle and set my foot against the jamb of the door, fumbling with the pipe in my other hand. It was like a baton, slick and moving between my fingers.

"That you, Will Besting?" came a voice through the small crack that exposed the other side.

It was him. Rainsford. His voice was ominously calm.

"You know I'm stronger. You better just start running."

I held the door with one hand, but I was losing my grip as the gap grew larger.

"I've got all the time in the world."

I hated his voice, hated it so much I wanted to open the door and hit him in the face with the pipe. But I knew better. I had a burst of new energy, an adrenaline-filled rush of power. The door pulled shut in my hand

and I slid the pipe into place, jamming it with a forceful thrust that left me breathless and shaking.

Rainsford was contained, at least for the moment.

I yelled and jumped up and down like a little kid.

"You okay, Will?"

It was Ben behind me, who was turning out to be a guy who was terrible at following instructions.

"Yeah, Ben. I'm okay."

"I really didn't want to go back in there. Can I just stay with you instead?"

I smiled, even laughed, and put my arm around his shoulder. The blue light blinked on and off again and the beeping sound returned.

"I have a better idea," I said, guiding Ben to the bar jammed in the door. "Hold this bar right where it is, don't let it slip."

Ben took hold of the bar just as Rainsford tried to pull the door open. It held nicely, but I could see how the bar might come loose and fall to the floor if Rainsford tried ten or twenty times.

"Sure, Will. I can do this," said Ben. "And Will?"

"Yeah?"

"Get us the hell out of here, will you?"

"Working on that," I said, and then I was running

again, hoping to make it back to the observation room before I'd been missed.

═══ ═══

The first thing I noticed was how quiet it was. I took a few seconds to just drink it in—the calm of the room with all the monitors off except the one at the main entrance. That one delivered a cold, silent view of nothing moving. I took a deep breath and held my hand over the S4 feed.

Time to check in with Kate.

When the feed appeared she was standing there, looking bored and beautiful. She was in profile, staring at the floor, but she knew I'd returned.

"How'd it go? Save the world again?"

"Maybe not the whole world, but it went as planned. We're still in the game."

"Glad to hear it. Connor called over a few minutes ago. Still nothing from behind the door. Maybe Alex and Avery are making out."

"Somehow I doubt that. Hold tight, okay? I'll leave your monitor on in case something comes up."

"Roger that," Kate said. She was starting to sound like

Connor as she rubbed her temples. Kate was tough as nails. I could see why people would follow her around, and for a brief moment I wondered what would become of her.

Kate Hollander, CEO of a large corporation. Yeah, that fit. *And a marathon runner.*

Maybe I was thinking about things that really didn't matter because I was apprehensive about what I'd see when I clicked the S5 feed on. It was the one feed that had returned nothing but a wall of darkness since I'd arrived in the observation room. I knew what was hidden in the dark, I just didn't know if I wanted to see it.

I engaged the S5 monitor and found that all the doors in the room had been opened up. Two people were in there, scanning shelves, looking for something.

"Hi, Alex. Hi, Avery," I said as softly as my voice would allow. I didn't want to scare them into dropping something important.

Alex turned around, but Avery did not. Her hair and clothes were wet and it looked like she was shaking.

"Will? Hey, Will!" said Alex, moving closer to the screen. His clothes were wet, too, but his short-cropped hair had dried.

"How many vials?" I asked, getting right down to

business. Avery still wouldn't turn around. As Alex looked at the wall of open doors, I shuddered at the thought of what I saw. So many vials, all lined up in rows. It couldn't be.

"I don't know, man. I think about a thousand. It's a lot."

1,000 vials divided by 6 equals . . .

Alex could tell I was calculating the enormity of it.

"I know, crazy right? I did the math. If it's seventy years for every six vials, he's about twelve thousand years old."

"But that's impossible. I mean *totally* impossible."

Avery spoke without turning around, and what she said chilled me to the bone.

"They're not all his."

Avery turned around then, her ghostly face even more troubling with the strings of wet hair hanging in clumps over her eyes.

"There are others like him, there have to be."

It was as if she'd been thinking about this idea a long time, running her fingers along the vials and wondering, calculating. Could there be more than one Rainsford out there? It felt impossible. It was also an idea that had the power of distraction, which was something we no longer had the luxury of enjoying. It was Kate who reminded us all, as her voice boomed into the observation room from where she stood at S4.

"Focus, you guys, focus! Or let me in there and I'll get the job done. Who cares if there are more Rainsfords running around? All we care about right now is *this* one. Seven vials, that's it. Get them and get out."

I was reminded once more as Avery touched the pocket of her soaked jeans that it was she who carried the seventh vial.

"Took a while, but we finally figured out they were lined up in order. Ours were the last ones in," Alex said. "We found 'em, only there's a problem."

"Let me guess," I asked. "You only found six."

Alex looked at me like I could read minds and nodded.

"Goring said she had to keep hers, remember?" Kate yelled. She trained her eyes on the one person that mattered. "Avery?"

Avery wouldn't answer as Marisa arrived next to Kate. She'd heard Kate yelling and wondered what was going on.

Avery Varone wouldn't speak. She went back to the wall of a thousand vials and I wondered what she was thinking.

"Avery, listen to me." It was Marisa, with her soothing, sleepy voice. "I know how much you love him."

"No, you don't," Avery said without turning around. "You don't know anything."

"But I do. And I know how much it hurts when they lie. I know how hard it is to trust them again."

It stung to hear Marisa's words, but there was nothing I could do. My betrayal was being played out in front of everyone whether I liked it or not.

"He loves me," Avery said, and I could tell she was crying. "Only me. No one else."

"You might be right, but either way, he's keeping things from you. Big things. I know how that feels, too."

"And he's sorry," I added, partly for Marisa, but more for Avery so she'd understand. "Listen, Avery. Please. This is about us getting cured. You can make that happen. If he really loves you, he'd want that for you. He'd want you to help us, wouldn't he?"

Avery didn't answer as Alex held up six glass vials— three in each hand—and mouthed the words, *What do I do?*

I could tell him to tackle Avery and take the seventh vial. She was crafty though. She might figure out a way to make sure at least one of them broke or got spilled.

"I think you're right," Marisa said. "I think he does love you. *Only* you. And I don't think that's going to change if you help us."

I glanced at Kate's monitor and saw that she was staring at the floor, wincing in pain. The stress was finally getting to her. Those headaches were getting worse. Marisa looked utterly exhausted. I was having trouble hearing everyone. Even Connor, with his rock solid persona, wobbled back and forth in a distant blur on the monitor, one of his spells coming on unexpectedly. All of us were—in one way or another—in need of a cure. And if Mrs. Goring was telling us the truth, Avery had what we needed.

"Why are you guys soaking wet?" I asked. There had been a brief lull in the proceedings and it was a question I'd wanted to ask.

"Wet?" asked Marisa, because she couldn't see them from the angle of her monitor.

"Yeah, so once you get past the X door there are some steps getting in here," said Alex. He was happy to have something to do besides stand there and look stupid. "First there's this tube and a ladder that goes down, a lot like how we got underground to begin with, then it's like a beach with water coming up to the edge. The room we're in is on the other side of an underground lake. And let me just say it is some frickin' cold water. I don't recommend getting in if you don't have to."

It wasn't really a lake, I knew. It was a missile silo, filled with groundwater. That was the round part I'd guessed about on the map. And behind that, the room with the vials.

Avery came toward the camera, and to my surprise she pushed Alex out of the way and put her face right up in the lens. Up close she looked more innocent, and I was angry at Rainsford all over again for what he'd done to us, to her.

"Marisa?" she called. "Are you there?"

The two of them had talked many times during our first visit to Fort Eden. They shared things we couldn't have known about. They had been like two peas in a pod.

"I'm here, Avery," Marisa called from the passageway. She, too, came up close into her screen.

"Get out of the way, Will," Avery said, and I realized I was standing between them, blocking their views of each other. When I was out of the way they stared at each other for a moment. It was the first time Marisa had seen her, and I could see how badly she felt for Avery, how surprised she was at the hollowed-out girl on the monitor across the room I stood in.

"Will you come in here?" asked Avery. She glanced at the floor and back up again. "I can't do this alone."

There was no hesitation in Marisa's answer.

"I'm going to the door, how do I open it?"

"Give me five."

Avery crossed to Alex and talked with him, saying things I couldn't hear. He looked in my direction as if searching for an answer, but Avery commanded his attention once more and he stared directly into her eyes.

"What are you guys talking about?" I asked. "What's going on?"

Neither of them would say as I watched Alex hand all six of the vials to Avery and walk off camera.

"Whoa, wait a second—what's going on?" I asked. "Alex? Alex!"

I heard the sound of moving water and knew that he'd gotten back into the underground lake of the silo. Avery wouldn't look at me.

What are you up to, Avery Varone? I thought. I still didn't trust her and now she had all seven vials. If she'd wanted to, she could destroy them right there in the room. She was alone. She could throw them against the wall, smash them to bits.

I felt helpless and alone. My team was spread out all over the place, my girlfriend was on her way into the deepest, darkest part of the facility, and the most unstable among us was holding all the vials. I almost wished Mrs. Goring would return and started to wonder why she hadn't. She'd been gone longer than usual—forty minutes, an hour? Her absence made me nervous the more I thought about it.

Nothing was happening that I could see, which felt like a lull before a storm. A bad omen. I thought about visiting Ben, just to make sure everything was okay at the door, but decided against it when Connor came running up to the S4 monitor.

"Did you approve this thing with Marisa? Why don't I go instead?"

"Avery wants to see her," I said. "I think it'll be okay."

Secretly I worried that Connor might get in that freezing cold water and seize up on us. He'd drag Marisa under with him and they'd both be dead. I knew Marisa could make it because I'd seen her swim back home. She was solid, she could do it.

"Just wait for them to come back. We're almost out of this thing."

"You mean she's letting us out? No way! Why didn't you say that?"

I couldn't bear to tell him the truth, but Kate made sure he knew without me having to say anything.

"No such luck. His master plan doesn't include us getting out of here. At least not yet."

Connor scowled at me, like I'd lied to him or told a half-truth, and then walked away. When he vanished into the hallway leading to the X door, I started watching the S5 monitor again. Avery was somewhere off camera, probably at the water's edge waiting for Marisa to show up, and I stared at the rows of vials. Could there really be a thousand vials of fear blood? It sure looked like that many.

"Where's Ben?" Kate asked.

"He's holding the bar in the door so Rainsford can't get out."

Kate just nodded. It looked like it was taking some effort to speak at all.

"Bad?"

"Yeah, not great. It must be getting dark outside. That's when it's the worst, right before dark."

"I wonder why."

"Couldn't tell you. Maybe pain and darkness like each other."

I had been right about the bad omen, the calm before the storm, because right when Kate said those words, everything started to fall apart.

It started with Amy, who unexpectedly returned to the main monitor. Her cheeks were flushed, as if she'd been running or gotten embarrassed.

"Will, she knows! You have to get out now! She knows *everything*!"

"Slow down, Amy—what happened?"

"There's no time, Will! She knows and she's going."

"Going where?"

"I did what you asked. I unlatched the way down. I even opened the door and left it that way. But she *knows*, Will. She's leaving right now. And she's mad. Like, *really* mad. At you."

"Can you stop her? Slow her down? Anything?"

"I can't even get out of here! I'm locked in the basement. You have to get out now, Will. Get everybody out. You have to save me."

Amy started crying. She was really scared, like a beast was lurking outside the bomb shelter door, trying to get in.

"Hold tight, I'll get there as fast as I can. I promise!"

There was a voice from the basement—was it Mrs.

Goring? I thought it was, but I couldn't say for sure with my rotten hearing. Had to be, because Amy gave me a look before she killed the signal that said something important:

She's not gone after all. I'll keep her here as long as I can. Go! Go! Go!

This was at least a glimmer of hope. *Thank you, Amy!* was my first thought as I focused my energy on the S5 monitor. Looming up in the back of my mind was time. It was always about time, it seemed, not enough or way too much in the case of Rainsford. It was about a six- or seven-minute walk to the pond, but Mrs. Goring was in the basement and she had to make sure everything was locked down tight so no one got out. That could take, what, five minutes extra? I had a max of twelve minutes to get everyone out, which meant Avery and Marisa had to be on the other side of the underground lake within five at the most.

"Marisa! Answer me, it's important!" I yelled. Kate stirred from where she leaned hard against a wall.

"What's wrong?" she asked.

"Hang on—Avery? Marisa! You need to leave, *now*. The doorway out is open but not for long. We don't have much time!"

"Coming!" yelled Kate. She was getting out of the missile silo whether anyone else made it or not. "I'll grab Alex and we'll meet you at the exit. And Marisa and Avery? If you can hear me, and I know you can, get your asses in gear! It's time to move or get left behind! And don't show up without the vials. I mean it!"

I appreciated the extra boost of enthusiasm from Kate as Marisa's flustered face appeared in the monitor.

"We're coming! We talked it through, and we're coming!"

"Do you have the vials?" I asked. I had no illusions about Mrs. Goring helping us, but if we could just get out and escape into the woods before she found us, it wouldn't matter. We could take the vials home and do the work ourselves.

"Swim fast! Run faster!" I yelled. "There's seriously like *no* time. You gotta move."

Marisa didn't even take the time to answer me, she was just gone. And then Avery appeared in the screen. She had a wisp of a smile on her face, which I hadn't seen all day. She seemed almost happy.

"We'll make it. Don't go leaving without us."

I told her I wouldn't think of it, and then I double-checked to make sure the red zone door was open. I was about to leave the observation room when a thought raced to the front of my mind.

What about the seven candidates in Fort Eden? Are we just going to leave them behind? What about Amy?

I wasn't responsible for all of them, but I did feel responsible for Amy. She had talked about going first, which could mean really, really soon. If Mrs. Goring got Amy drugged or under some kind of deep hypnosis or whatever, I'd never forgive myself. And the other six candidates were trapped, too. How fast could I get the cops up here? It would take a few hours, at best. It wouldn't be fast enough.

I saw two dripping-wet figures come into the tunnel on the S4 monitor—Marisa and Avery were out—and they were running. That was my cue to get to the exit.

"Will, over here!" yelled Connor. He and Kate and Alex were running up the red zone tunnel. One of them had a flashlight, and it sent a dancing beam of light in my direction.

"I'll get Ben," I said, and ran for the blue zone, where I found Ben sitting on the ground, holding his back with one hand and the metal pipe with the other.

"You okay?" I asked.

"I'm good, but he's pissed," Ben said. He stood partway

up and started hobbling toward me on his sprained ankles. "I think he'll keep unlocking the door and banging on it until it falls off its hinges."

"You're probably right. Just one more good reason to get out now."

"For real? The door's open?"

"Yeah, I did it. Let's go."

Ben threw an arm around my shoulder and I helped him walk back toward the entryway. When we got there Kate, Connor, and Alex were milling around, nervous energy having overtaken them. Seeing Ben, Connor went into commando mode again.

"We got an injured guy on our team, let's get him out first. I can go right behind, catch his weight if he starts to fall."

"Fine by me," said Kate. "I think I'll wait a second, make sure my girls get out first."

Ben was all too happy to start up the ladder before Kate even stopped talking, but he wasn't fast enough to beat Alex to the first rung. He was flying up that ladder before Ben could take his first step. Once he got going, Ben hopped from rung to rung, making slow progress, and Connor pulled up behind him.

"What's the plan at the top?" Connor asked. "Do we

just go right out or wait?"

"I think we scatter and run for the cars. Just get out and run; we'll do the same."

Connor nodded down at me like he was raring to go, but he was nervous. He kept looking up into the tunnel like it was spinning around in circles.

"Feeling dizzy?" Kate asked.

"Nope, I'm good."

Connor began the slow ascent to the top and Kate nudged me on the shoulder.

"Don't go in there until he's out. You don't want to end up under a falling football player."

Kate could be cold, but she had a good point. Beneath a free-falling Connor Bloom was not a place I wanted to find myself.

"If we do get cured, he's so going into the army," I joked. "He's already trained."

"Yeah, he'd be a natural."

Nine minutes had passed, and I didn't want to tell Kate we were down to almost no time by my calculations. It was altogether possible that Mrs. Goring was already standing outside waiting for us with a shotgun as it was.

I heard a noise in the distance, down the red zone

tunnel, and I couldn't help myself. I started running in Marisa's direction.

"Go ahead," I said to Kate over my shoulder. "You might as well. We're going to make it."

Kate looked in both directions and seemed to weigh her options.

"No thanks. I want to see those vials for myself. Plus Connor's not to the top yet."

I could see the resolve in Kate's expression when I looked back once more. She'd come this far to get rid of a constant, blinding migraine. She wasn't about to take any chances.

There was no reason for me to run toward Marisa. I just wanted to. I wanted her to see how much I missed her, how much I loved her. How proud I was of her getting Avery to come along. I rounded the corner at the S1 station and kept on going.

"Marisa? Avery?" I shouted. "Come on, fast as you can!"

They blasted through the red zone door, soaking wet and shivering despite the run. Marisa saw my silhouette and knew it was me. When our bodies connected we hadn't slowed down quite as much as we should have, and I think it nearly knocked the wind out of her. I wrapped my arms around her shaking body and felt the clammy cold of her bare neck on my lips.

"Are you getting me out of here, wonder boy?" she whispered, close and shivering in my ear. It was pure magic. I didn't even answer, I just took her hand, made sure Avery was with us, and started running toward the exit.

I kept looking back, making sure Avery was there. She was slower than I would have liked, moving more at a jog, and finally I slowed to a walk.

"Can you go any faster?" Marisa asked, and Avery did pick up her pace, but not enough. I felt sure we were already out of time and Mrs. Goring would lock us in all over again. When we finally reached Kate she already had one foot on the first rung, nervously looking back and forth between us and the way out.

"They're already outside!" she shouted. "It's open up there, I can see it."

At first I couldn't believe it was true. Had Amy really come to our rescue, opening the latch so we could escape from a maze of horrors? The idea surprised me, and I didn't believe Kate until I pulled in next to her and stared up into the shaft. At the top there was a faint circle of light, the light of a day coming to a close outside.

"This is good," I said.

"No duh," said Kate, but I was thinking not so much of our escape, but of what we were escaping *into*. It would be easier to slip away at nightfall than it would have been in broad daylight.

"Ready to get out of this hellhole?" Kate asked Marisa, and then to Avery: "You have what we came for?"

Avery and Kate had never been very close, in part because they'd briefly fawned over the same person. Young Rainsford—Davis—had caught Kate's eye, too. I had the feeling as I glanced at Kate just then that she didn't exactly feel sorry for Avery.

Looks like getting the guy wasn't such a good deal after all. Sorry that didn't work out for you.

"I have all seven vials," Avery said softly.

"Let me see them."

Avery didn't like being bossed around and narrowed her eyes. She wasn't about to give in to Kate Hollander that easy. In the shadow of a fight over a guy, the two were rivals above all else.

"Where's Davis?" she asked, looking at me then, thinking I was the most likely to know.

It was a hard question to answer, one I knew was coming. She wasn't going to leave the missile silo without him.

"There is no Davis. There never was. And Rainsford is going to betray you."

"You don't know that," Avery said, but it wasn't force-ful. The spell was breaking in his absence.

Marisa touched Avery's porcelain white hand, holding it delicately.

"He tried to kill me, Avery. Me and Will both."

Avery began to shake her head slowly as her gaze shifted to the floor. We had to get out before the door slammed shut and locked again, but Avery was crying. She was confused and upset, but we couldn't leave her behind. I was afraid she might run back into the dark-ness of the tunnels, screaming Rainsford's name, turn-ing her back on us in the end.

Marisa tightened her grip around Avery's hand. They looked like two young children about to wander into a forbidden wood with only each other to depend on. The way they looked at each other, there was some-thing deeper that hadn't been there before, something I couldn't understand.

"Let me take you out of here," Marisa said.

Avery looked up, red eyed and sallow. "I can't do it. I can't."

"Then give me the vials and stay here if you want," said Kate. She'd had about enough of the Avery weepfest to last her a lifetime. "Stay down here, be my guest. But you're giving me those vials one way or the other."

Kate was taller and stronger than Avery, towering over her like an oak tree.

"We can't make you come with us," I said. "But we want you to."

Kate took one step toward Avery, which put her about two inches from punching her in the gut (something I could actually imagine Kate doing in a situation like this). Avery reached into her back pocket and pulled out three vials, but she wouldn't give them to Kate. She handed them to Marisa instead.

"Hold these," Marisa said, passing them off to me. Feeling their delicate glass casings made me nervous about having charge over them. They were each filled with a black gunk so thick it smeared all of the glass inside. Throughout this exchange Marisa and Avery had not stopped holding hands, but now they did, and Avery dug three more vials out of her other back pocket. These she handed directly to me.

"Yours is in there," she said, wiping the tears from her face.

My fear in my hands, and everyone else's, too, I thought.

"Where's the last one?" Kate asked, still not backing down as she glowered over Avery. "Come on, Avery. You have a death wish, fine. But that door isn't going to stay open if Goring finds out. Give me the damn vial!"

Avery dug down into her front pocket and pulled out her vial.

"I hate carrying it around anyway," she said. "I'm not even sure why I need to. He just said so, and that's what I did. Because I do whatever he says."

She said the last part without sincerity or sarcasm. It was said flatly by a girl on the verge of falling apart, and this made it impossible to say where her true allegiance fell.

"You take it," Avery said, giving her vial—the seventh vial—to Marisa. "Don't let it go."

"I won't," Marisa promised, and just like that, Kate was climbing up the rungs.

"You're stupid for staying down here," she yelled back. "I thought you were smarter than that."

It was, in its own way, the kindest thing Kate could have said. She was clever enough to know a challenge between rivals might get Avery moving.

But it did not.

A few seconds later it was Marisa in the shaft, and then it was me. I took one last look back, wishing it wasn't true.

"Are you sure about this? You might not get another chance," I pleaded.

She wouldn't answer—only nodded—and hearing Connor yelling down the tunnel made me realize I had to get him to shut up and fast. He was drawing attention to us, and half of our number weren't even above ground yet. Kate was moving like lightning, already to the top before Marisa was halfway. Three rungs on my own journey to the top I heard a noise I hadn't expected. It was the kind of noise that makes a heart stop, a noise with the power to bring misery.

In hindsight I should have thought it was possible. I should have planned for it.

Ben wasn't there to hold the pipe any longer. And even with my terrible hearing, I could hear it when the pipe hit the hard tile floor. It was a sharp, metallic sound, followed by the ringing echo of the blue door being slammed shut. Avery hadn't opened the blue door, she hadn't needed to. He'd finally done it on his own.

Rainsford was free.

THE FINAL HOUR

We'd arrived at Fort Eden about one PM. An hour later we'd found Mrs. Goring, eaten some pancakes, and heard about the vials. We'd gone to the pond and made the mistake of marching down the ladder. We'd spent six hours underground.

That last hour would change everything in ways I would not have imagined possible. Much would happen in the final hour, and it began with our escape from the underground missile silo. I had long since given up the idea of getting out alive, so it came as a weird sort of shock when I arrived at the very top of the ladder and smelled the warm forest air outside.

"I thought we agreed you were going to run for the cars," I said, seeing Connor lean his head down into the round space. He wobbled as if he might fall.

"Back off there, tiger," said Alex, pulling Connor away from the abyss. "Let's get everyone out before we start falling in."

"That Avery behind you?" Connor asked as my head cleared the opening and I hopped out onto the floor of the shed. I glanced down into the hole, unsure what to do.

"Yeah, it's her. And *him*."

"What? That's—I thought he was, you know, *disposed* of," said Ben.

Rainsford called up from the bottom, where he was just mounting the first few rungs. "No sense locking the door. I'm coming out either way."

"No such luck," I said, but I didn't have to. Everyone heard the gravity of Rainsford's words ricochet through the air. And even though the latch on the iron door had held him this long, I don't think any of us believed it would stop him now. He had that kind of power in his voice, the kind that could blow through walls and locked doors. Somehow, he'd get out. He'd find each and every one of us.

"You guys should go, seriously," I said. "Start running for the car before Goring shows up with a gun."

"We're not leaving without you." It was a voice I knew but kind of didn't. I'd only ever heard it through an old monitor with sketchy audio. I had two things attached to the sides of my head that passed for ears, but my hearing was so crummy I still couldn't be sure.

"Amy?" I asked, and she came through the door of the small shed, concerned but smiling. She was far more beautiful in person than she had been on screen; downright breathtaking. Her eyes were sharper, her hair softer in the light forest breeze, her skin radiant. It was like going from a regular screen to HDTV and finding a bunch of treasures hidden in all that extra detail.

I was speechless, unable to find the words to express how thankful I was for what she'd done or how awkward it was for us to be standing in the same five feet of space.

"Should I shut this thing or what?" Alex asked, breaking the silence. He was standing behind me, balancing the heavy door on its hinges.

"No doubt about it," Kate said. "At least until we figure

out what the hell we're doing. We can always let them out later."

I held a hand up, signaling Alex to wait as Kate looked coldly at Amy like she didn't trust her. Marisa was also staring at Amy, seeing how pretty she was, sizing her up, trying to figure out if this new girl was going to be a threat or not.

"Avery, can you hear me?" I yelled.

"She can hear you fine," Rainsford answered for her.

"Go back down," I replied, feeling emboldened at my position in relation to his. "We're thinking."

I had this other, unexpected feeling as the door started to slam shut and Rainsford's protests were cut off in midsentence: I was trying to impress someone, to act like I had things under control. It was Amy I wanted to impress, and I felt a pang of guilt at the thought of it.

What's wrong with me? I thought.

I'll tell you what's wrong, bro. There's a heavenly creature standing three feet from your face and you're playing hard to get. What are you waiting for?

Keith, you don't know the first thing about having a girlfriend.

Whatever you say. Amy is hot though, you gotta admit.

The wisdom of little brothers is endlessly entertaining

and dead wrong most of the time. But knowing these things didn't cause me to stop staring at Amy. Marisa sure did, though.

"Is there a plan, Will?" she said, but she didn't take her eyes off Amy. "Like shouldn't we be getting on with it? You know, *leaving?*"

Alex pushed the heavy metal handle into lock position and stood up, slapping his hands together like he'd just completed a very difficult and important task.

"It looks crowded in there," Amy said from the door. Marisa had been looking at her, but Amy was pretty much settled on looking at me, which is probably why Marisa broke into the open space on the dock and nearly knocked Amy out of the way. By the time everyone was outside standing in front of the pond, I felt like I'd lost control of the situation. Connor was having one of his dizzy spells and sat down hard on the wooden dock. Marisa stared out at the water, arms folded across her chest, as far away from me as she could get without stepping into the pond. Amy was staring at me like I'd betrayed my promise to ditch the group and wander off into the woods with her. Ben was hobbling around like a crippled old man while Alex and Kate stared darts into my forehead that basically said, *Get it under control, Will. What are we doing here?*

I zeroed in on Amy, feeling time compressing against our odds of escape.

"Where is she? Where's Goring?"

"You wouldn't believe it if I told you."

"Try us," Marisa said, but she didn't stop looking at the pond.

"Wait—this is important," Amy said, and she was moving like a flash back toward the shed. "You're not going to believe it—just hold on."

"Amy, what are you doing?" I asked her, and then I started to get a sixth sense that we should start running, just leave and never come back.

But Amy looked at me with those piercing eyes and asked me once more in a soft voice, "Just give me one second, okay? I promise, it's going to be fine."

"What do you have there, Amy?" I asked.

"That's it, I'm leaving," said Kate. "Marisa, give me the vial. We'll mix up our witches brew at home."

"You got the vials? All of them?" Ben asked. He'd taken to sitting down, wincing in pain, which was only part of why I was feeling compelled to stay. Connor was just coming out of a severe dizzy spell and Marisa, finally turning in my direction, looked so worn out I didn't have much faith in her making it all the way back to the cars without needing a good long rest. At best I could hope for a few of us to escape, a few of us not to. It wasn't the kind of outcome I would willingly choose. I was, for better or worse, at that low self-preservation point where I believed it was all of us or none of us. It was starting to feel more and more like something was terribly wrong and we were all about to perish. Amy was only in the shed for a few seconds before she came back out. She had a smile on her face and her hands behind her back like she had the most amazing surprise hidden there. It was something she could hardly wait to share, and I got a morbid vision of Mrs. Goring's severed head held in Amy's hand. It was a vision I had to shake free from, a doomed vision even I had no interest in seeing come true.

But why? Why did I feel that way? What marvelous secret was Amy hiding that felt somehow all wrong instead of all right?

"I'm sort of sorry, but not really," Amy said.

And that's when Rainsford came out of the shed, holding the metal pipe I'd used to hit him not once, but twice. Amy had pushed open the lock on the hatch, letting a beast loose into the world. That was her surprise.

"Amy, what have you done?" I asked. She was standing exactly halfway between the dock, where we had all gathered, and the shed.

No one else spoke. No one moved.

Amy turned in the direction of Rainsford, the two of them catching each other's eyes at the same moment in time. I could no longer see Amy's face, but I could see Rainsford's. I could see a long-forgotten memory appear in his mind and bloom as a full-blown revelation on his face.

"Eve?" he said.

"The one and only," Amy said.

But it wasn't Amy. There had never been an Amy. It had only ever been Mrs. Goring all along. My mind, and that of everyone else who knew Fort Eden the way I did, understood what was happening in an instant. It was one of those wonderful tricks of the mind—the way it can calculate so much in the blink of an eye—the way everything falls together.

"How did you do it?" I asked, the first to speak, though I had a pretty good idea.

Rainsford took a step closer, like a man who hadn't seen his young lover in a very long time, trying to decide if it was really true.

"Seven hours instead of seven days," Mrs. Goring said. "Same result, it's just a little more complicated. Nothing I couldn't handle."

She'd had seven new subjects, ones we'd never seen, and she'd done their cures before we arrived and while we were belowground. Each hour a new one, each hour turning into Amy or Eve or—whoever—the point was she turned young again, but only for a little while.

She'd known all along, every step of the way, all that was happening underground. She'd been Amy *and* Goring.

"You look even better than I remember," Rainsford said, taking one more step closer, tentative but excited.

"There's twisted and then there's *twisted*," said Kate. "This is insane."

Rainsford and Mrs. Goring were both young again, and as the shadows of night began to fall on Fort Eden, every angle told the same story: an old feeling was new again. Rainsford was in love.

And this, above all other mistakes he could have made, was the one that *did* have the power to undo him. A shotgun, a metal pipe, a frozen pond, a floor of radioactive waste—all of those things paled in comparison to the power of a woman scorned. For young Eve

Goring had let out more than just Rainsford, she'd also let out a ghostly-looking girl named Avery Varone. With night coming on, she really did look more like a ghost than a living, breathing girl as she crept silently closer to Rainsford.

"Davis?" she said, when she had come up directly behind him. For a moment he wouldn't turn, so captivated was he by the sight of young Eve Goring. It was a moment he would come to regret as his fatal mistake. It told Avery everything she needed to know about the man she thought she knew. She was the one with something important hidden behind her back, not Eve Goring.

As Rainsford finally did turn to look at Avery, it came to me. I knew what it was before I watched Rainsford hold out his arms to embrace Avery one last time. Alex was the one with the pouch filled with insulin shots, but I hadn't seen the pouch in quite some time, not since he swam across the water into the room of vials.

Avery Varone had taken some precautions of her own. She was going to be ready if Rainsford ever betrayed their love. I think it was me that saw the needle first, but it might have been Eve Goring. She was closer.

Avery accepted Rainsford's hug, putting her own arms around him, and when she did, the needle went into the meat of his shoulder and she squeezed out the seven parts of blood swirling around inside. My blood, from my fear, and the blood of everyone else: Alex, Connor, Ben, Kate, Marisa, and Avery. It was the perfect poison, the one thing that could end the unending.

Rainsford knew. As sure as he knew his own name, whatever it had been at the beginning, he knew: death had finally found him.

The horror of decay shivered across his body and hobbled him to his knees. He looked at each of us in our turn, the knowledge of doom spreading on his face.

"The final mystery comes to me now," he said, and in the time that the words passed his lips, he aged twenty years.

Eve Goring—or Amy—posed a cruel question. "You never loved her, did you? I was the only one."

But Rainsford had more pressing matters to attend to.

Death was on him. He had no time. Twenty more years passed in the span of Eve Goring's words. He was creeping up on sixty in a hurry.

"I loved no one," he said, but I knew it was a lie. He had loved them both, but more than that, he had loved himself.

He was eighty, wrinkled and old as Mrs. Goring had

been, his back curled in an arc that forced his face to the ground. The pipe fell out of his hand and rolled into the wild grass of the wood.

"Well, for whatever it's worth," Amy said, and she did seem like an Amy to me, young and dominant, "I never loved you, either. I always thought you were a little on the dumb side."

God, she was so beautiful! I could see how Rainsford would have fallen for her. Strong like Kate, cuning like the Goring we knew, yet soft like Marisa. A horrible, powerful beauty.

The very last went quickly, just as dusk turned to night in the forest and the air began to chill. There was just a little light left, enough to see a man go from eighty to one hundred and beyond. Things accelerated after that. All the death Rainsford had managed to avoid landed square on his face as he lifted his head and screamed in terror at the coming night of his soul. Small craters punched into his face, his eye sockets deepened until there were no eyes at all, and dust began to fall.

Death had found him at last. Turning him to particles before our very eyes. Even the bones blew apart with a harrowing *pop!* that seemed to fill his empty, wet clothes with air. Only the shirt and the pants and the shoes remained, all else was turned to dust in the shadow of Eden.

The man was gone, but Eve remained. An Eve of destruction, or so she must have thought.

"Were you ever going to cure us?" asked Marisa. She had moved without my really paying attention, without any of us knowing, to within a few feet of Mrs. Goring. Mrs. Goring turned to face Marisa. It was hard not to think of her as Amy when I looked at her, though I could see the same mocking spark in those eyes.

"I'm not as cruel as you might think," said Eve. "If you have the vials, you have your cure. I was telling you the truth. Assuming Avery was smart enough not to use it all, you got what you came for. Mix it with some water. It will cure what ails you."

——— ———

We did not leave Fort Eden until the next morning, because there was work to be done and records to be gathered. We destroyed all the mechanisms used by Goring and Rainsford—anger therapy of the finest variety for each and every one of us. And I discovered tapes from monitor and audio feeds, things I later used to build a narrative of everything that had happened underground. It was the darkest part of the night before our work was complete, and I sat with Marisa on the same couch where I first met her. It was an unusual late evening for at least two reasons. For one, Marisa was wide awake. I missed the warm limbs and soft breath I had come to know so well, but the chasm of silence was filled with the second reason the night was so unusual: I could hear *everything*. Small creatures moving in the forest outside, feet padding along the floor, the whispers across the room. Even the sound of mist gathering on the tall trees did not seem to elude me.

"I don't know, I sort of liked you better when you were half deaf," Marisa whispered.

"You weren't bad asleep, either. Less chatty."

"You're funny. And gross. You were kind of falling for an old lady."

I pulled Marisa close and felt her soft skin.

"You have to admit, she was kind of a knockout as a teenager. But you're cuter." She sat up straight and took my hand in hers. Something about the events of the day fell heavy and tired in her eyes, and for a second I thought maybe she wasn't cured after all.

"I'm going to love you just the same when you're old,

Will Besting. Don't go letting me down."

I pulled her up, kissing her with a new kind of confidence I hadn't felt before. But what could I say that would make her feel safe? What would any girl want to hear that they could actually believe? Would I be there when she was ninety? Would we even remember the moments that shaped our lives together, drawing us down, ever closer to death's door? I told her what I could: that I knew the secrets of Fort Eden, that I knew her heart and my own, and that we would go down fighting together.

"Not bad," she said, pulling me toward the door. "Come on, I've got energy to burn."

By the time we got outside Marisa was reenergized. In the deep night of Eden, we listened to the world around us and the rhythm of each other's laughing, and felt the wonder of being alive, just the two of us.

═══ ══

More time has passed. Some things I know better, some questions still remain. Of these things I am sure:

The apparatus for conducting the fears has been destroyed. This was mostly Connor with the metal pipe, a job he wanted sole ownership of, though he could not withhold at least a few swings from each and every one of us. Some parts have found their way to the bottom of the pond, others are smashed to bits and pieces. A thousand years of science or magic or both are now fallen into ruin.

Our vials cured us of what Rainsford took away. Why he wouldn't have just let us have those cures to begin with I don't know. It is a very peculiar being who wants suffering in the world purely for the pleasure of it, and I don't claim to understand what makes it bloom in an otherwise normal human being. I will say this: to let suffering endure needlessly will blacken the kindest heart over time. Maybe Rainsford began only as a heartless man, not a wicked one. Maybe having no heart and a lot of time leads only to the abyss in the end. Who can know the ways of a man after his nine hundredth birthday? They get complicated at that age.

I feel very happy for everyone. Kate is radiant and less angry, much more prone to laughter than she used to be. Not having a splitting headache will do that for a person. Connor is captain of the football team again and he has, as I suspected, joined the ROTC. He has every intention of becoming a Marine, and I think he'll be a good one.

A great one, actually. Alex is just "better," which is to say I don't really keep up with him too much. I suspect he's happier without the fanny pack and the needles. Avery has made a full recovery, and she is probably Marisa's closest companion if Ben isn't around. Ben and Avery, a couple, something I would not have predicted. But then again, they're similar in spirit: reserved, lost, hopeful, confused. And they came out of the experience damaged more than the rest of us. They saved each other in the end, it seemed to me, willing each other to get healthy.

Mrs. Goring did, indeed, discover a way in which to use the fear chambers and the machinery at Fort Eden to work Rainsford's black magic on herself. When we arrived at Fort Eden, there were seven participants hidden away in their own basement fear chambers, awaiting their moment. They never knew what hit them, and by the time we escaped from the underground missile silo someone had already taken them all away. But I'm getting ahead of myself. Mrs. Goring went from Amy back to herself over and over between cures. When she was Amy, she called as Amy. When she was Goring, she called as Goring. It was only Eve Goring all along.

"I got what I wanted," Eve told me before we left.

She was sitting by the pond again, staring at the pile of clothes that used to contain Rainsford.

"What was that?" I asked her.

"I outlived him. It was worth it just to see him fall head over heels for me again. Priceless."

"Being sixteen isn't all it's cracked up to be," I said. "You might not like it as much as you think."

She smiled mischievously, as if I had no idea what I was talking about.

"Here, so you can save the world again. You're getting pretty good at it."

Eve gave me a list of names and addresses, along with seven vials. I made it my special mission to find the Goring seven, to make sure they got cured of whatever disease they'd picked up at Fort Eden. "You could have killed us down there," I said. "It was wrong what you did."

Eve stared at the pond with those piercing eyes—eyes that were much too sharp for a young girl. "I'm not a sorry person, never have been," she said, and I felt the bitterness that had settled in her bones. It was a bitterness she would die with, I knew. "You got cured and Rainsford is dead. We both got what we wanted."

It's 10:30 PM and Marisa is still awake, playing video

games with her sister while I lie on her bed half asleep. I can hear every sound they make. And there's another voice, a closer one, deeper inside.

I have to admit, that whole Amy/Goring thing had me fooled. I wouldn't have bet they were the same person. Gotta give Goring some credit—she did in seven hours what Rainsford needed seven days to accomplish. She was only Amy for, like, fifteen minutes at a time. Crazy.

Good thing you've got me to watch over you, bro.

Yeah, good thing. That's your job though, right? Big brothers are supposed to know this stuff.

Yeah, it's my job. I got it covered. Air hockey?

Now you're talking!

I drifted off to sleep, the sounds of Marisa and my little brother laughing until I couldn't tell for sure which of them was dead and which was alive. But life, I was coming to find, was like that. There were things a person couldn't be cured of, like falling in love or missing a lost little brother. I carry them around like glass eggs and hope I don't drop them, because those are the things that make me who I am. The things I won't let go of.

When at last I face the specter of death at my side, the deep-down things are all I will have to comfort me.

They are who I am, who I was, who I will be.

FEAR IS THE CURE
DARK EDEN

Immerse yourself in DARK EDEN with the multimedia version for Apple and Android.
Free app download.

- Download the 2D bar code reader software with your phone c
  http://enterdarkeden.com/app/reader

- Take a photo of the code using your phone's camera.

Text DARKEDEN to READIT (732348) for more!
U.S. Residents Only. Message and Data Rates May Apply.

KATHERINE TEGEN BOOKS
An Imprint of HarperCollins Publishers
www.enterdarkeden.com